D1269865

HIGH COUNTRY ADVENTURE

By the Same Author

Devil's Doorstep
The Seal of Frog Island
Shipwreck Bay

WEEKLY READER CHILDREN'S BOOK CLUB

presents

HIGH COUNTRY ADVENTURE

by Marian Rumsey

illustrated by Joseph Cellini

William Morrow and Company
New York

For my husband, Bill

Contents

CHAPTER ONE

In Back of Beyond

I hadn't wanted to come in the first place. There was to have been a blast of a birthday party for my friend Johnny in his folks' apartment on Nob Hill, and now I would have to miss it. Actually the trip was Father's idea, and I hadn't been able to get through to either him or Mother how disagreeable it would probably be.

We were flying at ten thousand feet, though the pilot of the little plane, Sam Murphy, said we were actually only about eleven hundred feet, more or less, above land. I could believe it was less; he was skating over tops of mountains and skimming edges of cliffs, all too close to suit me. I hadn't flown much before, and then only in big jets complete with first-run movies at the flick of a switch. Seldom had I even bothered to look out the curtained port. I did now, and I was nervous.

We were in the heart of Canada, heading north. There was nothing in sight but a blanket of trees dotted with bright blue lakes, and all speared by sheer peaks top-heavy with snow, as far as the eye could see. I thought the country was one of the most desolate-looking areas imaginable. Until then I hadn't realized there were parts of the world so completely uninhabited. I was George Allen, a city boy who had no interest whatever in the great, wide open spaces.

"Isn't that one of the prettiest sights you've ever seen?" Sam asked. However, I wasn't the slightest bit interested in his big colorful country so I just answered with a grunt.

Father had written to Uncle Henry about my visiting him. He and Aunt Min had some sort of homestead in Canada, on the fringes of Alaska, and Father practically forced them to take me up there for two weeks. I didn't want to go. I guess I managed to irritate everyone thoroughly trying to refuse. But Father was stiff about it and insisted I needed Uncle Henry's firm hand for a while. That remark meant I'd overgrown my haircut again, and my friends were breaking things up around the house more than usual.

When I finally got back from all this good, wholesome fresh air, I'd have to go to school. My last few weeks of holiday had to be spent taking long, invigorating hikes observing nature with Uncle Henry, and I would have to be well-mannered, too. Father thought that if I got out in what he called the high country, I might shake loose some of my high and mighty ways. I think Father actually liked the place.

"Does this thing always cough and gurgle so much?" I asked, as the plane made unusual engine noises.

"Well, she's not a 707 jet, you know," Sam said, annoyed. He had been irritated ever since

I got aboard. I suppose that was because I'd told him his plane looked as if it were held together with Scotch tape and string.

Then, just before we left, he had called a giant of a dog that had been roaming around the airfield. The beast lifted up his dark head and looked me over thoroughly before leaping inside the plane.

"Is he going?" I asked.

"Of course."

"But he's a dog!"

Sam looked at me with disgust. "Rather."

What I'd meant was I thought a dog simply didn't ride in an airplane like a passenger, that he ought to be in a cage. But I was lectured about how this particular dog was part of the airplane and went everywhere, so why didn't I just sit down, buckle my seat belt, and be quiet. And, oh yes, the dog's name was Ami, in case I had to talk with him.

I didn't particularly care about Ami sharing

14

my seat, but I hadn't much choice. He was big
and black with long, floppy ears and huge feet.
Every few minutes he slipped over to rest
against me, and I had to keep shoving him
aside. Each time I did his tail plopped pleas-
antly, bashing me in the face. On top of everything else he was wet. I'd seen him wading in
a little stream by the airport, and he smelled.

Early in the flight, in a more affable moment,
Sam had told me that he had been flying for ten
years and had taken over his grandfather's flying
service. He ran flights all over the bush, deliver-
ing supplies, mail, and even hunters into the
high country. I wondered if perhaps he had in-
herited his grandfather's plane at the same time,
but surely it wasn't as old as all that. Still, even
for a bush plane it seemed a bit dilapidated.
However, Father had made this same trip earlier
in the year, so I guessed it was sturdy enough.
Trust Uncle Henry to have settled in the back
of beyond, where the only way in was by the

smallest airplane in Canada or by footing it with a pack on one's back.

"Look at that river!" Sam exclaimed.

I looked down. It was as blue as the lakes and wound through the trees like a snake looking for a way out of a thicket.

"I say," I muttered again nervously, "this plane certainly does a lot of sputtering." Even the dog had come to life, sitting up now, poking his dark nose against the glass and leaving a wet smear.

"Yes," he agreed, "it does sound a bit—" the plane made an unsteady swoop "—sick?" He laughed heartily. "But there's nothing to be alarmed about, kiddy."

Well, that did it. I'm going on thirteen and don't like being called a kiddy.

The plane gave another cough. I could feel a sudden loss of speed, and I automatically held my breath. Then the motor caught, and I relaxed and breathed again.

"Really now, this. . . ." I looked at the landscape below. "I mean—it *is* going to get us there, isn't it?"

"Fuel problem, I think," he said. And at that the motor sputtered for the last time and stopped completely. "Blast!" he fumed. "Seat belt, kiddy. Just might have to put down for a bit."

I jerked myself out of whatever sort of horrified trance I'd been in and did as I was told. I heard the whine of the wind for the first time, and the plane felt sluggish as it settled toward the ground. Anxiously I looked around the horizon for some open spot where we could land, but couldn't find a place at all. Sam was muttering to himself, working furiously to get the engine restarted.

We were losing altitude fast, then we banked sharply and I saw the river swooping up. It didn't look so blue now; it was speckled white with choppy water.

"There's a spot," he said calmly. "Put your jacket and those sleeping bags in front of you.

17

Cross your arms over them. Ami! Down off that seat! Might be a jolt. Can't tell yet if the sand's firm."

I had my coat in place and my face protected even before he finished. I felt the plane list suddenly, then straighten. We were coming directly at the treetops like a locomotive. The tiny strip of open shoreline along the riverbank seemed far, far too small for a landing. I heard a scraping, scratching noise, then a screaming and ripping. There was a crack of timber and the crashing sound of metal and glass. I felt a great weight jerk around my middle, and with a final tremendous lurch we stopped.

I wasn't the least bit hurt, only breathless and terrified. I pushed the jackets away. Three or four suitcases had come unstrapped from behind us and were lying on my head and shoulders. I untangled myself and the dog, then pulled myself over the seat and crept beside Sam. He had a nasty-looking bump, which was bleeding some, over his eye, but he wasn't un-

conscious. Ami was already scrambling past me to reach him.

"Get out," Sam told me, but I could hardly hear the words. Without thinking, I managed to help pull Sam upright in the pilot's seat.

"Blasted leg's stuck," he shouted in my ear. And I could see that it was badly wedged below his knee. I reached down in the twisted wreckage to find what was holding his foot. There were strips of metal and wires, all in one great mass that seemed to have no end.

"Pull," he shouted. "Down, Ami, down. Pull, George!"

Well, for pity's sake, I was pulling. I yanked at the wires tugging them away, but at that moment the plane gave a sickening heave and with another grinding of metal it fell to one side. I rolled away and bashed my head on the instrument panel.

"Ah. It's freed. Well, don't just sit there kiddy! We're sinking!"

Only then did I realize we had skipped over the little beach and landed in the river. I pulled myself up to look out the window. The water looked rough and mean, white with rapids as it hit broken, fallen trees and ugly sharp-looking rocks.

"Glory!" I said stupidly.

"Push out the window with that suitcase," Sam ordered. "Don't try the door, let in too much water."

I shoved the case through the glass that was already broken, and managed to get the frame cleared. Then I shoved my head out the window all the way. There was a clean, wet smell of foamy water mixed with the sharp tang of pine. The sun was very bright, reflecting from some strip of metal on the tail section that was twisted back nearly double on the fuselage. Despite all the land about, we had been isolated in the center of the river.

"Fine how-de-do," Sam offered half-apologetically.

"Do you suspect the river's very deep?" I asked.

"Don't know. We seem to be moving a little. Probably have to swim."

"Oh, great!" I said miserably.

We looked around the cabin. It was a shambles. And though Sam must have been in some pain from the cut on his head, he was carefully packing a leather case with supplies. Then he put on his parka and handed me mine. Already the water was up to my knees and rising.

"Get everything out of those suitcases," he ordered. "Repack one with the things we'll need—food, medical supplies, and heavy clothing. It's going to be cold. Strap up those blankets. Hurry!"

The plane gave another lurch, the bow made an unpleasant dip, and I gasped.

"Can you swim?"

I nodded dumbly.

"Current's bad, but it's not far to the bank. The worst will be the cold. Leaving our clothes on will help, but it will feel like an ice cube so don't tarry." He laughed suddenly and wiped his finger over my cheek. It came away black with oil. "You could stand a bath, kiddy."

We hadn't time to repack the suitcase after all. The plane made another violent heave and water boiled around my feet. Suddenly we had to get out. Sam ripped a length of loose wire from the side of the cabin and tied his case to his belt. With another length he attached the two sleeping bags to Ami's harness.

"Out you go. Take one bag, but let it go if it gets to be too much. Don't put all your weight on that wing till I'm out. Must be deeper here than it looks—plane's settling."

I swallowed.

"You go first," he said.

I eyed him fretfully. "I'll get my watch wet," I said foolishly.

"Egad!" he roared. "Out!"

I knew the river would be icy and unpleasant, but I didn't realize it would be so paralyzingly cold. The water was over my head, and I had to swim. The current was very strong, and my first stroke pushed me up against the wing where I held on until Sam helped Ami into the water. Then he jumped and swam beside me. "Swim," he said, shivering. "Don't stop. You'll freeze!"

We struck out. Sam was a good swimmer, much better than myself. He had one suitcase in his hand, another on his belt, and he was swimming on his back. I had the smaller case, which floated very well and helped me some. I wished, though, I'd tied it to my wrist. It was slippery to hold, and I was trembling so much from cold I could hardly close my hand. Ami was doing some sort of maneuvering around the plane, swimming in circles, and I wondered if the fool had enough sense to swim for land. Then Sam shouted at him, and he turned to follow us.

I don't suppose the shore was more than seventy-five feet away, but it seemed like a million miles from us. My clothes became soggy and felt like lead. My shoes filled with water, and my feet got so cold they had no feeling at all. Wherever the water touched skin it was like a burning flame, and that was ridiculous because it was freezing cold, not hot. I was sick and so tired that I could hardly breathe.

Then I felt hands on my shoulder and looked up to see Sam leaning over me. I let my feet sink and found the water was shoaling; I could stand waist-deep. On the bottom were round, smooth stones, which rolled underfoot like marbles, followed by thick, sticky mud, which sucked at my shoes, finally pulling one completely off my foot. I had to go underwater to find it, and for a moment the overpowering noise of the river became a muffled quiet. The world around me turned a greenish-blue filled with crystal bubbles. Then I surfaced, shoe in hand, and stumbled shivering on the bank, falling flat out in the tall marshy grass.

I had expected to be even colder out of the

water, but I wasn't at all. In fact, once I caught my breath, I was almost warm.

"The suitcase!" shouted Sam. "Quickly!"

Glory! I'd forgotten all about it. Now it was drifting away. I leaped to my knees, snatched for the case and missed. Getting to my feet, I lunged and missed it again. I fell in the water with a gigantic splash that succeeded in really pushing the case into the current. Then I high-stepped after it and somehow got tangled up with Sam. He shoved me to one side, and I sank like a brick.

When I came up he was chin-deep, but had not managed to save the suitcase. He staggered back toward me. "If you would keep out of my way. . . ." Sam said irritably. Then he stopped knee-deep in the river. Ami had made it ashore and had begun to bellow—not a bark, but a howling wail that echoed beyond the tops of the trees.

"Ami!" Sam shouted, pointing at the disappearing suitcase. The dog was instantly back in the water and swimming after it like a shot. Only a minute had gone by, and he was close enough to make a bite at the case, but he couldn't connect with smooth airline plastic. He snapped again, but all he collected was a mouthful of water.

"The handle!" Sam shouted. "The handle!" As if the dog could understand, I thought to myself. About five snaps later Ami found the handle, or rather the luggage tag, and with it clamped securely in his teeth headed for shore. But he was nearly in the main current, and some nasty-looking white water was shooting around an overhang of rock close by.

"He won't make it," I said.

"Ah," said Sam, "but he will."

I'll admit that Ami was a great swimmer. I realized he must be a Labrador and probably enjoyed the water. But suddenly he was caught in a flukey swirl, and both the suitcase and dog made one quick whirling orbit. Never losing his grip, Ami just managed to get into the lee of the rocks. At last he reached calm water and stood up. Turning, he pulled the heavy case with strong shoulders and a vicelike jaw until it was out of the water. All this time he was still dragging the sleeping bags tied to his harness. Then he let go and looked upriver at us. His tail was wagging furiously, as if to say smartly, Look at me. He shook himself, then raised his voice in that deep bellow.

"Good boy, Ami!" said Sam, as he took me by the arm and pulled me up the bank. Then he went straightaway to Ami.

I'm not sure what would have happened to me if Sam hadn't been around, or if he had been killed in that crash. The thought of my being alone just then was the most frightening thing imaginable. I hadn't liked Sam Murphy from the very start. Even though he'd tried to be nice enough, I'd been irked about being in Canada and had been doing my best to make his life as miserable as mine. I was sorry now, honestly, because I realized how close he had come to being killed. I looked out to midriver. All that was left of the little bush plane was a silver tip of tail sticking out of the water, looking something like a foamy rock.

I stood there shivering as he brought up the bags and case and put them all together by a fallen tree. He told me bluntly that he hadn't been able to get out a Mayday on the radio. At the time the engine had begun misbehaving, the radio had also failed. So I was brought up rather sharply to the fact that we were stuck in the middle of nowhere, hundreds of miles from civilization, without hope of being rescued. I wasn't so foolish as to think someone might spot us from the air through the heavy carpeting of trees. Two people marooned beside one of thousands of streams and rivers without the small aid of a plane's reflecting metal—why we would be no more visible than a needle in a field of wheat.

"We might as well be on the moon," I said shakily.

"Well, yes, in a way. This part of the country isn't exactly overrun with humanity."

"We'll never get out."

He grunted and began feeling the lump on his head. "We aren't so far from people as you would think," he said thoughtfully. "A couple of miles over there is old Jud McCoulough. He has a little cabin at the foot of those mountains. Trapper, I guess you'd call him. Hardly ever packs out."

"You were trying to land near his cabin, weren't you?"

"Um. Pass me the medicine chest. That's a good kiddy."

"My name's George," I said. I opened the chest and took out some alcohol and gauze bandages. I dabbed where he told me and mopped and taped. When I finished, he looked nearly as good as new.

Suddenly there was a great crashing of underbrush just beside us. Ami began the most terrific roaring, and my hair must have stood on end. "What's that?" I yelped, leaping to my feet.

Sam was putting on dry boots and never even looked up. "Maybe it's a bear," he said shortly. "It's all we need to finish up the—"

"A bear!" I guess my mouth dropped open like a stranded fish. "Glory!" I'd seen a few bears in my life, but all in a cage at the San Francisco Zoo. To meet one in the flesh was certainly the last thing on earth I wanted just now. "Oh, for pity's sake," I said furiously, "that's not a bear. It's a man."

And an ancient man at that. Hobbling out of the bushes, he looked nearly a hundred years old. He was weathered and worn, his eyes sparkling out of a wrinkled face, and his dirty white beard reaching almost to his waist. So thin that his patched clothes hung on him, he looked like a wizened scarecrow.

"By jibbers! If it's not Sam Murphy. By jibbers!"

"Jud!" Sam got to his feet laughing. "Jud, I

didn't expect you to come find us." The meeting was glorious with lots of backslapping and handshaking. One would have thought they were long lost brothers the way they carried on.

"Thought for a minute there you were going to pass me by. What did you do with that fine-looking airplane? Heh-heh!" He cackled like an old hen. "By jibbers it's good to see you! Come to stay awhile, eh? Heh-heh! And who's this fine-looking laddie?"

"My name's George," I repeated sourly. Then after an explanation from Sam I was slapped on the back, too. Apparently he knew Uncle Henry—everyone seemed to have heard of him. Uncle Henry wrote books, and every few years came out of the high country to give talks at universities and schools about the flora and fauna of the Far North. Why Sam even knew Uncle Henry and Aunt Min so well he had spent a week with them earlier in the year.

"By jibbers now think of that," said Jud, shaking his head. "This laddie is an Allen.

Say, Sam, you know I was fixing dinner when I saw you two sputtering around in the sky. Thought for a while you were going to aim for my meadow, but guessed you hadn't the altitude. Say, haven't got a little smoking tobaccy on you, Sam? Heh-heh!"

Sam packed up the rest of the things and began searching through the bags. I had some tobacco I was taking to Uncle Henry, but I didn't have a chance to offer it to Jud. Sam just handed the lot of it over. "Better see if you have any dry shoes," he said to me. "No need walking in those wet ones and blistering your feet."

The suitcases had kept things remarkably dry. I would have liked to change all my clothes, but they were waiting to start for Jud's cabin. Then I caught Sam staring at the shoes I'd found to put on. "Those aren't exactly meant for hiking," he said unpleasantly. They were short, buckled black boots with pointed toes and high heels.

"So what," I said. "They're all I have."

The three-mile trek to Jud's cabin was miserable. We saw a thin trickle of smoke above the trees long before we ever saw the cabin itself. Then we had a little stream to cross, which was tricky since I had to do it barefooted holding my shoes over my head. Each stone and rock seemed to have some sort of sharp edge that jabbed my feet like knives.

Once across the stream we came to a well-used path. The dog, who was forever running in and out of the brush, making an infernal nuisance of himself, finally let out a yowl and with his nose pressed to the ground took off up the trail. In a few minutes we came out into a clearing.

Jud's cabin, if one could call it that, wasn't put together much better than Jud himself. The smoke was coming from a hole in the roof, which was part of a hill rising up behind it. The rest of it was made of sod, grass, and dried weeds, and there was a bush on it nearly three

feet high. The main part of the cabin was built into the mountain itself with only its face exposed. The porch was held up by some rickety-looking logs set at all angles. On one side a supporting timber had fallen out from under and that corner had caved in, leaving an untidy pile of dirt and growth just outside the door. The cabin front was a collection of odd-sized logs, as uneven and burry as the day they had been felled. Grass grew here and there where the timbers had been chinked with stones and bits of earth.

There was one window, covered with a dirty-looking piece of canvas. And as I watched the canvas fluttered slightly and a raccoon jumped to the sill and sat down to look at me. Ami let out a moaning sort of whine, and I rather thought he was saying hello to the little fellow.

"That's Jacques," said Jud, hurrying up and throwing open the door of his cabin. Then he smiled, displaying a set of toothless gums, and welcomed us to his castle, which smelled of smoke and fish. He had been cooking a fish stew, and it turned out to be amazingly good. There wasn't a lot—he hadn't been expecting visitors—but we all had enough.

Later he and Sam sat around the fire talking over what was to be done with me. The first thought was that I could stay with Jud while Sam went for help. Jud's cabin, though not exactly the Ritz, was his home, and he seemed to have managed to survive in it for the past twenty-two years. He even showed us his ice-box cut into the mountain and his cold cellar under the floor. Both were very well stocked. He told us that his Indian friends had done his winter buying this year, and he hadn't left the area at all. Nowadays he was slightly arthritic, and since the Indians liked to look after him, he let them.

I perked up when Jud mentioned Indians, thinking they might have trucks to take us out. But the local Cree, who were hard to find, traveled their routes and worked their traplines on foot. Furthermore, at this time of year they were settling in for the winter. Certainly they could not take the two of us out to civilization. I was downcast to learn how few people lived in this country, and how purely fortunate we were to have crashed nearly in the lap of one of them.

They sat there for a long time, puffing on crooked cigarettes made from Uncle Henry's tobacco, until Sam's popped open in the middle and spilled into his lap. He jumped up and slapped it into the floor grinding it out. The floor was earth, covered spottily with grimy-looking skins. The little raccoon was sitting in the center of one, delicately licking a fish bone. He held it in his two hands, turning it and enjoying it. Then he carefully laid it aside and picked up another. A pile of bones was stacked beside him, within a few inches of Ami's nose. The big dog, his eyes like glistening honey, his tongue smacking at his lips, lay there watching him. I'm not sure whether he wanted a chance at the fish bones himself or perhaps a meal of the raccoon. But Ami was well-mannered and only occasionally glanced toward Sam with rather longing eyes. When he got a stern look in return, he simply sighed, put his head back on his big webbed paws, and watched.

"It's absolutely out of the question!" Sam kept saying grimly.

"Now, now," said Jud. "You can't expect this laddie to stay here. You know the chances of getting snowed in."

"I certainly do," Sam said vehemently. "I also know my chances of getting him to his uncle's place if the snows come while we're on the way."

"Posh!" said Jud. "Won't be a heavy snow till middle of the month. Signs are everywhere. Besides you've made the trip before on the river, and except for one bit it's easy."

"Posh, indeed."

"Now, now," soothed Jud again. "You can

both be at Henry's in a week. Then you can pack out yourself from there with their mule. If you go south from here, think of the pass you'll have to cross. No. Wouldn't want you two stuck up there. If you get snowed in at Henry's, well—be kind of fun. There's those that likes to winter in you know. Now take this laddie's aunt and uncle. They tell me the best time of year for them is winter. He does his writing. Min, she gets all her miniatures caught up."

Aunt Min does dinky little oil paintings that are so small they could fit in the palm of her hand. Uncle Henry carves the frames, some of them not much more than a few inches square. She is always back on orders from some fancy New York gallery that sells them for her.

"Think of the chess you could play," Jud went on. He slapped Sam on the back and nearly sent him reeling. "Say now that's a dinger idea. Heh-heh!"

"But won't planes come searching for us?" I asked.

They looked at me, and I slunk lower in the corner, sorry I'd opened my mouth.

"Kiddy, I wander all over the great Northwest when I fly a plane. They wouldn't have the foggiest notion where to start."

"Isn't that a bit dangerous?" I said sharply.

Sam nodded. "Reckon so. First crash I've had though—in let's see—five years. That time I flopped down on the field in Nipigon. Mud was so thick I nearly sank to China."

"Why don't you want to take me out?" I asked suspiciously.

He didn't even bother to answer. The look he gave me was enough.

"Well, you said change my shoes!" I said furiously. "It so happens these are all I have." I was sitting on the floor opposite them. A bear rug beside me still had its head intact, and the yellow bared teeth gleamed unpleasantly in the

41

flickering light of the fire. Sam looked mad and tired. "And my name is George," I added sulkily. "Not kiddy, or laddie, but George."

The plans were settled. Sam was to take me on to Uncle Henry's, and from there he could go on out alone. Much against his wishes, obviously, but at least I was going. Somehow, just then, the trip seemed much better than staying in Jud's dingy cabin, where Jacques peeled fish bones.

The next day dawned clear and furiously cold. When Jud showed me the basin, where I could wash up, outside on the tree stump, he had to crack the ice to get to the water. I stood to one side huddled in my heavy parka that had dried out over the fire. I wasn't about to wash in that freezing water. Earlier I'd put a pot on the stove to heat, and I only hoped he wouldn't use it.

But he did use it for coffee, and I ended up following Sam and Ami down the path and did my washing up in the creek. Then while Ami ran off howling into the brush I sat on a stone and watched Sam lather his face and shave, a ticklish business. He was using a knife that must have been razor-sharp. I found out later he used that knife for everything, from nipping threads to slashing sapling pines for firewood.

My next unpleasant shock of the day was to learn that Uncle Henry was over three hundred miles away. This blow left me staring at Jud with my mouth open. Perhaps to him that distance wasn't far, but to a city boy it was two hundred and ninety-nine miles more than one should have to walk. Then a reprieve came. Jud had a canoe, and we apparently could travel in it.

The next disagreeable surprise was resigning myself to leaving behind all my treasures. Of course, I'd lost nearly everything when the plane sank, but what little I'd had in my case was most precious, or so I thought.

Sam sat cross-legged on the floor discarding everything worthwhile.

"Oh, now," I said for the nth time. "Not that."

"Look, you can't take a cap pistol in a pack on your back."

"I don't have a pack," I grumbled.

"Or a slot racer, or a monopoly set, or—" he looked slightly unbelieving "—a microscope!"

"I might see a bug," I said unpleasantly. I was exceedingly annoyed with him.

"But you can use this sheath knife," he admitted practically.

"That's not mine," I said, nettled. "It's a present for Uncle Henry."

He raised his eyebrows. "Well, I'm sure he won't mind your using it. Though I'll admit it's not quite your type, is it?"

"And what's wrong with my having a sheath knife?"

"Nothing, nothing," he muttered. "Only with your glamorous shoes and that choice hairdo, you really should have a switchblade."

"I don't think I like you."

Well, we got everything sorted. I did have plenty of warm clothes, heavy sweaters, and socks. Sam set to work sewing up an old backpack that was hanging from the beams overhead, and Jud had a better one I could wear; it was light and easy to manage. We packed them with our gear that evening under Jud's practiced eye. There wasn't much. Apparently travelers in the Far North carried no more than necessary—just extra clothing, a plate, cup, spoon and fork, a little stove, lantern, towel, and a bar of soap. Sam had the cooking tins, and I had Uncle Henry's knife. Jud had a lot of food he could spare, and it was divided and went in next. Then a sleeping bag was strapped to each pack, and we set out a small line tent.

Sam sent me to bed early, saying I was to have a good rest before we started. But I woke up during the night to something warm and heavy on my arm. I stared into the dark to see a small bandit face looking at me—Jacques had invaded my bedroll.

CHAPTER TWO

Down the Long Arm

It was not yet light when Sam woke me. Jud had a meal ready, a hot mush with undiluted canned milk, and it was about the worst start for the day I could think of. I didn't bother to go to the creek to wash, though Sam meticulously swung a towel over his shoulder and, with his bar of soap, left for a good scrub.

Afterward we loaded the canoe. Sam kept grumbling, half to himself, that the canoe was built for one person, not two and a dog, plus enough supplies for an army. We hadn't much freeboard when we all got settled, and Sam looked gloomier than ever. Jud was a little skeptical himself, but he slapped Sam on the back and told him to take it easy the first day.

Otherwise, we would both be back looking for sympathy.

Sam took the stern paddle, then asked if I had ever been in a canoe before. I chewed at my lip for a bit, said yes, once, in scout camp when I was eleven. He apparently deemed that experience enough, for he handed me a paddle and put me up forward.

Jud wished us *bon voyage,* and, just as we were ready to cast off, he took Jacques out from under his sweater and sat him atop our packs.

"Jud," said Sam firmly, "I'm not taking him along."

"Aw now, be a sport. Drop him off downstream somewhere. I can't get him far enough away to stay. He's getting ready to hibernate, and if he does he'll be underfoot all winter."

Sam shrugged. "Well, can't have you disturbing nature, I suppose. Good-bye, Jud. Take care of yourself." The farewell was rather pleasant. Ami barked sociably, and Jacques made a few revolutions around the packs, found a likely spot, and settled himself in, his little hands clasped serenely one over another. He and Ami began a staring-down contest, one that Jacques won out. Ami went to sleep; I'd found his special scratching place just behind his left ear.

The ride went smoothly down the creek and to the fork where it emptied into the Long Arm River. We came up to the remains of the bush plane. There wasn't much left, a few strips of fiber, which must have been attached some-where underwater to the fuselage, were float-ing downstream, but they were all. While we maneuvered in for a look Sam gave me short, brusque commands about paddling. I wasn't doing very well, and I could tell he was irritated and trying not to show so. Soon Sam gave a great push with the stern paddle, turning us about completely, and we set off downstream.

Then began what I suppose could be called the silent treatment. I'd known Sam hadn't wanted to take me, but I hadn't realized to

what extent. Not that I didn't deserve all I got;
I'd asked for it ages ago. I'll bet we traveled
nearly four hours, and he didn't make another
remark. I was facing forward, so I couldn't
really see him as I slowly dropped in exhaus-
tion. At times I crossed the paddle over the
gunwale and stopped completely to rest.
When I did I couldn't see much noticeable
difference in the speed of the canoe. My lack of
stamina irked me. Only once did I suggest we
stop for the day. I got a furious sort of negative
answer, so let it drop.

The Long Arm was a changeable river.
Sometimes it flowed wide and slow, a deep
greenish-blue, with eddies that swirled out
from the bank to touch us. The banks would
narrow in a while, the current would pick up,
and the bottom shoal. Before I knew it white
water would shoot up and around us, making
the canoe dance like a feather in the wind.
Then I'd hunch low in the bottom. I could only
hope Sam knew what he was doing since I was

absolutely useless. He did, for we always came out dry and safe, gliding along with the barest effort as the river fattened out again.

After the first few hours the banks thickened with brush until one could hardly tell where water and shore met. The trees grew taller, and the river ahead looked as if it tunneled beneath them. The mountains, topped with blinding white as the sparkling sun glistened on the snow, moved in. The country was awesome and, when the river was quiet, a little frightening in its stillness.

My reprieve from Sam's great silence came at lunch. He told me to fetch out the dried goose meat Jud had packed for us. I couldn't say it tasted much better than it looked, but it was chewy, and something to fill up the pit. He didn't bother to stop paddling more than five minutes, and we drifted. I could see little beads of perspiration on his forehead. I was cold, myself, and glad Ami was curled around my legs.

When the two animals smelled the food they both perked up, and Sam told me I could give a taste to Ami and a morsel to the begging Jacques. Ami inhaled his and drooled on my hand for more, but Jacques took a long time to eat. First he laid the strip of meat on the stock of Jud's gun, which we had borrowed and had lashed across the packs. Then he sat there just looking at it. I supposed he wanted to decide which was the best way to begin, since he had quite an undertaking to go through before he ever got it into his stomach.

First he tediously tore the meat into shreds. And, at last, with that chore done, he crept carefully to the gunwale of the canoe. Teetering precariously on its very edge, and hanging on with one paw, he rinsed the strip in the water. Next he scooched back up to the top of the pack, rooted about for a comfortable spot to sit, and ate. Then he went on to another piece and repeated the whole process once more. If he had washed the whole chunk at once, he would have simplified matters, but I suppose he had his own way of doing things. Afterward he wiped his face like a fussy old lady, made a few more revolutions around the packs, found another niche, and went back to sleep.

But we were off again. Ahead the banks glowed in a golden sort of fire, and as we came closer I saw the touch of frost. The sumac and dogwood, mingled with maples and aspens, were glorious in their bright coats. Leaves drifted from them even as we passed and fell with a circle of ripples. Picking up motion, they sailed downstream with us. But the blaze of color was only along the banks of the river, for on past were the pines, forever green.

My neck got stiff after a while, what with all my twisting and turning to look about. The voyage was like a Cinemascope travelogue in the flesh—mile after mile, hour on hour, of unending beauty. Uncle Henry would have been delighted. Then an icy blast of wind shot down from the highest valleys and set my teeth to chattering. I noticed the sun had sunk behind those massive pinnacles. The world suddenly seemed less pretty, more foreboding, and the trees looked dark and unpleasant.

Sam eased up on his paddle, and I turned around to see what was happening. "There's a spot for a camp ahead," he said. "We've come far enough today."

We rounded an outcropping of rock and slid into a sheltered little cove to a sandy beach. Beyond was a small meadow encircled by the forest. The wind was blowing across the grass waving and splaying it apart, and it looked lonely and cold.

I had to be told to unload the canoe, and by the time we had everything on the beach it was almost completely dark. I stood there and watched Sam set up camp. I couldn't help; I didn't know what to do. But in a few minutes he had most of the work finished alone, and I suspect he had done it a million times before. He cleared a level space back from the river, and then unrolled the tent. There was a small telescoped center pole, which he put in place and pulled up in the center. He drove in the corner spikes, and the whole works ballooned out. Next he disappeared into the trees with the ax. Ami let out a tremendous howl and went along.

By the time I dragged our gear within reach, he was back with a freshly felled young tree. He flicked off pine boughs with the ax and tossed them inside the tent until there was a fair-sized layer. When he had enough to suit him he spread a tarp over the lot, and we had a tidy floor. Then he threw in our sleeping bags, and I managed to get them unrolled and spread out. On top of them went the huge rabbitskin robe. By that time he had the lantern going and the primus stove set up on a canoe thwart that he had brought in the tent. He lighted the stove and put on a pan of water from the creek to heat. Next he built up a fire outside, got it alight, and soon the pan of water began to boil on the primus. He took it off, tossed in a handful of tea, and put on another pot filled with some of the goose meat and vegetables.

It was so cold by then that we couldn't stand it outside, so we came in the tiny tent and sat on the robe. The dinner cooking smelled delicious, and I was starved. It was warm, almost hot, and for the first time all day we peeled off our top layers of jackets and sweaters. Sam hung them from a line he strung crisscross across the tent top. With all our heavy clothes hanging about the tent was crowded, but somehow snug and homelike. That depressing darkness outside was forgotten.

"Are your hands sore?" Sam asked, as he poured me a mug of tea.

I nodded. "I'm afraid I wasn't a great deal of help."

"No. Not much."

I grinned. "May I row again tomorrow?"

"Paddle." He grimaced. "Not row. Yes, you won't be able to do much. Probably be sore as the devil." He handed me my tea. The steam blew up in my face. The tin cup was so hot it burned my lips, and I nearly dropped the whole thing in my lap.

"How far did we come?"

He shrugged. "Forty, forty-five miles."

"That much?"

"We should have done fifty," he said shortly.

"If I had been more help."

"Well, we have a big load," he admitted. "And for a boy," he added grudgingly, "I guess you did all right."

"That fast, we can be at Uncle Henry's in no time."

Sam grunted. He was mixing up some ugly-looking stuff in one of the cooking pots, then spooning it on top of the stew.

"What's that?" I didn't think much of it, whatever it was.

"Bannock."

"Is it edible?"

Sam turned to frown at me, and he looked a

bit fierce. His dark hair was long and hanging in his eyes. He needed a shave, and those blue eyes might have been shooting daggers at me—but they weren't. For a second I thought he would tell me off. Instead his eyes twinkled merrily, and he laughed. And from that moment on, Sam was my friend—for forever, I think.

The meal was really good. The bannock tasted something like dumplings, and it's a good thing there was a lot, because we ate as if we hadn't seen food for a week. Afterward I did up the few dishes while Sam went over the map. I sat cross-legged opposite him and watched as he plotted out our distance. There were lots of marks on the map, and I found out he had made this same trip more than a dozen times. Other parts of the map were covered with pencil lines, too, and I asked about them.

"I've flown them all, and I've walked them all."

"Do you really like this country?"

He looked at me for a moment, then nodded. "Don't you?"

"Good grief, no."

"Then what in the devil were you doing going up to Dr. Allen's place?"

"I hadn't any choice," I said fiercely. "Father told me to come."

Sam stared at me. I think he wanted to ask why I had to be forced into a visit, but either he decided that he didn't care enough or else figured Father was the only one with any sense.

"Have you been to Uncle Henry's place often?" I asked.

He nodded. "Often as I can. Your Aunt Min makes the best blackberry pie," he reminisced. "Last visit I stayed in the shed with Mortimer." Mortimer was Uncle Henry's mule.

"I can't understand anybody living up here," I said. "There isn't anybody. Or anything."

He chuckled. "Someday you won't say that."

59

Sam was wrong, or so I thought, but no need telling him so.

"What are you making?"

He had been busy over something ever since the meal was finished. He had leather and heavy cord in his lap. Now he stretched the material out on the sleeping bag and marked it.

"Shoes."

I blinked. "Oh?"

"Put your foot on this," he said, and I gaped at him.

"We aren't going to be able to paddle all the way, you know," he said shortly. "There's going to be a portage around the falls at Mastasi."

"But I have shoes."

"They will break your feet in about an hour, if you don't freeze them first. Put out your foot."

So I was measured for shoes, which left me feeling a little smug. They were going to be moccasins. Sam had learned how to make them from the Indians. One winter he had lived with a Cree family, trapping beaver with them. He must have learned quite a few tricks of existing on nothing, because they popped up at odd times and gave me a deep respect for Sam. I wished I could be as self-sufficient.

Ami returned from exploring and lay just outside the tent flap, and before long Jacques came picking at the netting. Sam said if we didn't bring him inside he would rip it, one end to, so I let him in.

I lay awake a long time that night, listening to the sounds of the forest. Sam must have been tired for he went right to sleep and began to snore. I heard Ami moving restlessly about outside the tent; once an owl hooted and was still. The tent smelled of pine and the oily fumes of the darkened kerosene lantern over my head. Then I felt the pad of little feet as Jacques did his evening gyrations at the foot of my bedroll.

I woke next morning as Sam shook me on the shoulder. He was up and had the stove going, but it was freezing cold all the same. I sat up groggily, and he handed me a cup of boiling hot mush. There I sat shivering while he poured canned milk and sugar over it.

It wasn't yet light, and while I pulled on layers of heavy clothes Sam started breaking camp. I loaded the canoe best as I could remember. Sam seemed satisfied enough. He pushed the gun under the strap on top of everything, and then told me to get aboard. I took the forward paddle, and Ami curled up in the center with the big rabbitskin wrapped completely over him. All he had showing were his nose and eyes. Jacques slithered up to the bow and sat in front of me, like a fat barrel, fingering the whiskers on his chin.

I had paid close attention to my instructions of the day before, so I knew pretty much what I should do to keep Sam from making any more remarks than necessary. Paddling wasn't as difficult as one might think, and even though I was stiff and ached a lot from the day before, I rather enjoyed it all. We hadn't gone more than a few miles when I saw something in the water just ahead. I shoved Jacques out of the way and leaned over the bow.

"It's a turtle," I said. I reached in the water and scooped him up before he had time to realize we weren't a floating log. He wasn't very large, about five inches long, and his color was a muddy-green. As soon as he came aboard, he popped back into his shell, and I could see he was not going to be sociable for a while.

"Any time you're ready," Sam said patiently.

I dropped the turtle into the bottom of the canoe and hurriedly picked up my paddle. Then Jacques got underfoot, because he wanted to investigate the new arrival. This movement upset Ami, who was under the robe, and for a minute there was a lot of motion up forward.

"I don't know what you're doing up there,"

Sam growled at me, "but around that bend there's a stretch of rather nasty water. I wish you'd get yourself settled."

"Okay, okay!" I said, trying to shove Ami back in the center and get Jacques up on the stempiece where he belonged. I wasn't really watching what I was doing, although I'd been warned. We shot around the bend, and if I had been more alert I would have seen how the river had narrowed and how the current had become tremendously fast. I readjusted my knee a bit and gave Jacques a shove with my elbow. When he didn't move I nudged him again. At the same moment Ami let out one of his roaring yowls that startled me into jerking upright. The noise must have terrified Jacques, who leaped straight up on my shoulder. Between my rather unsteady balance, and then the sudden eruption of white water on all sides—well, I suppose the inevitable happened.

"Get that paddle in!" Sam shouted. But somehow I had caught it against the bow, and as I gave it a tug, it flipped the canoe around at precisely the wrong second.

Sam roared, Ami bellowed, but I only gasped. The water very neatly flipped up and over the rail and swamped us so completely and so thoroughly that we never had a chance. The next I knew we were all sitting chest-deep in water in our same positions in the canoe. We came out of the white water into a long, smooth stretch of river something like a plane coming through the sound barrier into a great calm.

When I cautiously turned around I wished I hadn't. Sam had his hand pressed across his face and looked absolutely and hopelessly disgusted. Ami looked like a wet tepee with smoldering eyes.

"I—I'm sorry," I said inadequately. And at that Ami tried to stand up. Half-submerged as he was, he succeeded in completely upsetting everything, and we very, very slowly rolled over and upside down. Needless to say, we had to get out then. The water was only a few feet deep so there was really no danger. We fished out all our packs and gear; the gun, the food and meat, a wet raccoon. The day hadn't even dawned, and we were right back to where we had started—sitting on the beach around a fire.

Fortunately, the sun came out full and there was a breeze. Combined with four big fires everything dried out, more or less, by three in the afternoon. We loaded up again, everything back in place, but Sam pushed his fingertips on my chest and directed me to the center position.

"I'll paddle," he said firmly.

That night I wasn't especially popular, and I watched gloomily as Sam figured our meager miles gained on the map. "We didn't have a very good day," he said finally.

Admitting that we hadn't, I ate my stew and bannock in exile, and we hardly spoke to each other. Later he sewed on my new shoes and commented slyly that I'd soon be able to toss out my high-heeled boots. Finally I got so sleepy I couldn't stay awake. I made sure

Jacques was inside, that Ami was affectionately patted on the head, and that the turtle, which I had managed to save after all, was in a good spot in the corner. Then I went to bed and slept like a log.

I began paddling again the next day, and with an effort managed to keep my mind on my work. Things seemed to be moving along nicely, and about noon Ami set up a howl that made Sam decide to let him have a run ashore. We pulled alongside a likely looking log, which could serve as a dock, and tied up. Ami leaped out of the canoe and ran off into the tallest trees. I was forever wondering how he could always find his way back after being gone for hours on end. Jacques jumped out to the log, as though he were a bit stiff. He had spent all his time sitting on the tiny little section of wood that made up the top of the stem. Sitting down at the farthest end of the half-submerged tree, he stared into the water.

It was very still; this part of the river was like a looking glass. I wondered if he was admiring his rather silly face. I took my turtle ashore to let him walk in the grass. Sam put his fishing rod together, walked downstream a ways, and started casting. He was mumbling about the time of day being wrong and the sun not right, but he seemed to have hopes of catching something or he wouldn't have made the attempt. I stretched out in the damp grass and looked at the sky. I was warm, lying flat out, and considered removing a jacket, but the effort was too much. The day was lazy, and watching the thick clouds roll by was ever so relaxing. Soon I moved my head and saw the turtle climbing out of the walled prison I'd made. I shoved him back with my foot. Then I watched Jacques picking up little sticks and stones along the water's edge as he hunted for grubs. When he found one he hugged it to his chest, looking this way and that, as if expecting a monster to tear it out of his hands. Then he trotted quickly out to the end of the log, behind the canoe, to rinse it off and to eat in seclusion.

I must have fallen asleep, for when I opened my eyes again the clouds were blotting out the sun and a chilly wind went swooshing over me and set me shivering. Sam was back and picking stickers out of Ami's face. There were some cleaned fish on the log, so I guessed he had had some luck. I couldn't find my turtle for a minute, but he had only escaped behind a rock and was asleep. I scooped him up, made a ticking sound for Jacques, and got in the canoe. Then Ami and Sam followed, and we were off.

"Jud was wrong," Sam said, as we got into the mainstream.

"About what?"

"It's going to snow."

I looked up at those clouds again. They were thick and dark, and though there wasn't any wind it was getting furiously cold. Sam told me to pull up my hood tightly over my ears and to push the muffler over my face so nothing would freeze. My hands inside my gloves were cold, and I flexed them every stroke of the paddle. I got awfully stiff in the knees, but didn't move about much. I wouldn't want us to capsize now. We couldn't survive if everything was wet when the temperature was dropping far below freezing.

Because of the overcast, the day grew dark early, and Sam reluctantly stopped soon afterward. I could see a thin stretch of white water ahead reaching out in the weak last light, and I was glad that it would be daylight when we paddled through it. Though of course, I'd never have admitted so out loud.

The bank looked uninviting. The shore was thick with brush, and the trees hanging overhead were close and depressing. The one small clear area we found wasn't a good place, but it was the only one about. The current was strong right up to the marsh grass, so we made a foul landing, and Sam had to get his feet wet to pull the canoe inshore. Although the beginning of the evening was forbidding, it improved slightly when we built two big fires directly outside the tent door and were able to eat.

There was never much variation to our fare, but after the cold and the effort of paddling it always tasted good. After I washed the dishes, I dried Sam's boots on the ends of sticks until they smelled nearly good enough to eat. Sam kept on with his shoemaking. My moccasins were almost ready for the lacings, and I surely was pleased. He had a pair he wore in the evenings, and they looked very comfortable.

When his boots were dry, I coated them with oil and hung them among our clothes on the line overhead. The kerosene lamp sputtered sociably. We hardly ever went out to our evening fires, because it was always too cold. With the lantern and the little primus stove we kept warm and content inside the tent. Then I lay down and put my chin in my hands watching him. "I hope they fit."

Sam chuckled. "They will. Unless you've grown in the past few days." He looked at me thoughtfully. "No, I don't think your feet have, but I do believe you may have up here where it counts." He tapped my head slightly, and I grinned.

"How far did we come today?"

"About fifty miles, I'd think."

"A third of the way."

"The easy third," he said, handing me a moccasin. "See if that feels smooth on the toe."

"What's the matter with the rest of the trip?"

He took the shoe back and went on sewing. "First, it's going to snow."

"You're sure," I said slyly.

"Of course. Then tomorrow we should make the falls. If it's snowing badly, getting the canoe around will be misery. The portage is long, over five miles and not easy the best of times. Try that. If you can feel it with your toes, I'll change it." I slipped the thing on again and wriggled my foot.

"A portage," I said, "that's carrying the canoe, isn't it?"

"That's right. George, why don't you clean the gun." He handed me the necessary equipment in the box by his side.

I puffed up slightly. That gun and his ax and knife seldom left his sight. I did a good job, I thought, though he suggested I move Jacques, who kept licking the stock with his raspy little tongue, to one side. I suppose it was a little salty from handling.

"Whatever is the matter with Ami tonight?" I asked.

Sam bent forward and opened the flap of the tent. Ami half stepped inside and looked at our little gathering. Sam put his hand affectionately on the big dog's head. "Wolves," he said. "I imagine they're about."

"Wolves!" I gasped.

74

He nodded and closed the flap in Ami's face. I heard the dog go back and sit by the fire. In a moment he would be up again, pacing around the tent.

"Well, don't just sit there!" I squeaked. "Do something!"

He looked at me calmly. "What? They won't bother us. There's Ami. Besides, they're always around. Tonight they're just closer."

"But—they're wolves!"

He grunted and handed me a moccasin. "If you work the heel in your hand like this, it will be even softer."

I must have looked pretty well shaken up, for I certainly wasn't as calm about meeting a wolf face-to-face as he seemed to be. I glanced at the tent flap, half-expecting one to come in at any moment. "Is there a bounty on them?" I asked.

"Well, yes," he told me. "I suppose so."

"Do you kill them?"

"Why should I kill them?"

"They're wolves!" I gasped again.

Sam looked a little irritated now.

"You could make a lot of money," I said. "Couldn't you?"

"No!" he said sharply. "They don't bother me, and they have as much right to be here as I do. In fact, probably a bit more. I was born in Chicago; they were born right here in the high country."

"But they—they're killers."

"They aren't killing me," he said crossly. "Besides, there are a few killers in Chicago. I don't try to get rid of them."

I had to agree with him on that score. There are a few unsavory characters anywhere. "Will they hurt Ami?"

"No. But I'm going to make him sleep inside tonight and keep Jacques in. He would make a tasty dish. Jud has as much as murdered that animal."

I gulped. "What do you mean?"

"Mean? Well, look at him. Crawling all over us, curled up beside Ami half the time. He has as much fear for his life as—as—well, as you have." He scratched Jacques on the back, and the little raccoon looked up at him with soft, moist eyes. "One day on his own, and he will land in some animal's stomach."

"Oh, Jud must not have known."

"He knew," he said, stretching and yawning loudly. "He just didn't want to be the executioner."

I didn't go to sleep that night for a long time, and I turned restlessly on my bed of pine boughs. Although Sam was snoring away merrily, I heard sounds outside I'd never heard before. Each time Ami moved beside me to lift his head and listen, I did, too. A crack of a branch, and I was holding my breath. I had one hand on Jacques' tail. Once I must have given it a tug, for he let out a squeak. I tried not to think of the time he must leave us. And then, later, the wind picked up, and I could hear the low moaning of the pines. The sound was enough to make my skin crawl.

CHAPTER THREE

The Struggle

Ami woke us the next morning when it was barely light with an ear-splitting howl. I leaped straight out of my sleeping bag; my mind must have been still fresh with thoughts of wolves. I got tangled in the clothes hanging overhead and pulled them all down. Next the lantern fell with a crash, and our food supply scattered. I stepped on Sam, and Ami began to gallop around joyously. Jacques started to squeal, and I was terrified that my turtle might get trampled.

Then, somehow, I backed into the center pole and managed to knock it down. The tent collapsed, and the roof drifted down over us with an enveloping swoosh.

I hadn't much choice then but to sit quietly,

hands over my head, holding the suffocating canvas away. Ami was in ecstasy, either licking my face with his warm tongue or slapping me with his tail.

"I hope," said Sam, somewhere underneath everything, and in a most irritated voice, "you don't make a habit of this." He groped about for the pole and pushed it back in place; the tent blossomed up again. He lighted the lantern, and we could see the shambles. The oatmeal tin had popped open, and everything had a milky look. Ami was a dusty gray, and Jacques was fussily brushing his coat.

"What a mess!"

"Well, there's a bigger mess," said Sam.

I looked out the tent flap he was holding open. In the faint light of dawn I could see the snow, and I thought it looked pretty. The trees, which were thickly covered, looked like layer cakes. The ground outside was as smooth as velvet, until Ami let out a whoop and leaped out and across it. The snow was deeper than I expected; it must have fallen all night. In fact—I stuck my head out farther yet—it was still snowing. "Oh," I said, holding out my hand to catch a snowflake. "Look!"

Sam dropped the flap, but I pulled it back again. "Oh, it's lovely." The snowfall was the first I'd seen, and I was dazzled by the sight.

"A mess," Sam said again. He looked at the disgusting jumble inside the tent. "Everything's a mess," he said sourly.

I scooped up a handful of snow and threw it at a bush. The branches shook and scattered a cloud of fluff to the ground. Then I tossed a snowball at Ami, who had gone a bit wild in the head. He was racing back and forth howling at everything, enjoying himself immensely.

"It's so beautiful," I said again.

Jacques was sitting like a fat Buddha blinking out over the whole scene. He looked, like Sam, unhappy about the lot of it. He gingerly tried one foot, but the snow clung to it so he stepped back inside.

"Oh, you silly," I said. Picking him up bodily, I tossed him out. If looks could kill I'm sure I'd have been speared. Jacques stood madly beating each foot in turn, whirring it around like a propeller.

"You aren't a wild animal," I said, as he climbed back over the tent lip and snuggled into my arms. "You're a lap dog."

"If you would please close the tent," said Sam moodily, "it might get above freezing in here."

"I've never seen snow before," I said.

"Well, you haven't missed much," he said. "Scoop up that oatmeal before Jacques eats it. Don't be fussy. It's all we have."

After we started to break camp I began, at last, to see a bit of what Sam meant. At first I threw snowballs at everything and ran around making tracks in the snow, acting as silly as Ami. But when we had to start loading the canoe I found it wasn't so nice. Fortunately, we had put a tarp over the canoe, and it had kept the snow from getting inside. But when I went to fold it up Sam shouted, "Don't! Bring it by the fire and let it thaw out first."

Next I found that my gloves were wet from all my foolish playing and were unwearable. I used Sam's extra pair. He didn't make any suggestions, but I had learned my lesson. Then we began to launch the canoe. "Oh no," I said. "It's frozen in."

The shallows and marsh grass were covered with snow, and beneath there was ice. It wasn't very thick and made sharp cracks as it broke under the canoe. I got in the bow, smacked a paddle at the surface ahead of us, and listened to the scrape of slush against the sides. Suddenly I was glad the canoe was aluminum. Surely those knifelike splinters of ice would have cut any fabric. Then we were away from the bank and the ice, and almost at once the canoe swung with a nasty jerk. Sam put all his strength to work and got us in place for the white water ahead.

We had been in rapids before; usually they lasted a few minutes and made a short, bumpy ride. But this time they were the beginning of a spine-chilling trip. The rocks and ledges piercing the water were capped with snow and it was nearly impossible to tell white swirls of water from solid stone in the distance. I thought, time and again, that we would crash head on into an outcropping of rock. Once we came so near I let out a squeal of horror, but Sam had us past before I had time to think. I worked like a demon. Occasionally Sam shouted an order to me, and I surely hoped I was doing the right thing. The roar of the river was deafening.

Then like a shot we rounded a bend in the river, and I was shocked at the sight ahead. Instead of improving, the water beyond was even more violent. Foaming and boiling, the river narrowed until it was but a gorge. The wet, slippery-looking cliffs on both sides were dotted with lonely bracken covered with snow.

The river looked mean and cold and very dreadful. I turned to gasp at Sam, but he didn't pay any attention to me. He looked ferocious; he hadn't shaved for ages, and his dark hair was hanging in his eyes. He had pulled his cap over his ears, the collar of his mackinaw high. Suddenly he smiled in a way that he seemed to save up for only the most special times. I felt immeasurably better and turned back to paddle. I was so tense I could hardly sit still, and my nervousness must have passed on to the animals, for they were restless.

Then to make matters worse it began to snow even more. Instead of spotty flurries thick snowflakes fell, and we could hardly see. In a matter of minutes the canoe was solid white. My dark parka and hood were covered, and I must have looked like a snowman. I could feel Sam move about in the stern. He couldn't see far ahead, but he couldn't stop—there was no place to land. We hit a swirl that swung us nearly broadside to the mainstream, and I was so near a huge, wet rock I could have reached out and touched it. But we flashed on past with hardly more than inches to spare. As soon as we were pointing properly again, I made out an abrupt hook in the river, and we raced at one face of the gorge with the speed of an express train.

Sam swung his paddle, and I felt the icy splash of the water as it sprinkled on my face. We didn't look as though we could make the turn, and I looked hopelessly at the solid wall towering over us.

There was a boil of foam where water met rock, and for an instant we were caught on its top and whirled like a dervish. I heard the heavy grunt of Sam's breath as he fought the weight of the canoe. We rolled precariously close to capsizing. Although we didn't go over, we took a few buckets of water over the gunwales—and most of it hit Jacques.

Up until that moment the little raccoon had been relatively still. But with a sudden icy bath he moved away from my knees and up to the rabbitskin robe. At that very moment the canoe swung abruptly in the other direction, dipping horribly. Jacques made one, futile attempt to catch at the rail, and he fell. I tried to snatch him and missed. The canoe must have run directly over him as it twisted, narrowly missing the cliff.

"Jacques!" I screamed. I tried to see the animal in the foam astern, but I couldn't and screamed again. Ami pushed himself out from under the robe. He had seen Jacques go over. His dark eyes looked sharply one way, then another. And before I realized what was in his mind he was up, over the side of the canoe, and had disappeared into the river as completely as the raccoon.

"Ami!" Sam shouted hoarsely, but what with the gigantic lurch as the dog went over, we had all we could do to get the canoe straightened for the next twist of the gorge.

I don't know how long it was before Sam

found a spot to stop. I never even noticed it, but I suppose experience had taught him that behind the great point of land erupting from the canyon would be a lee for us. We rounded the headland like a bouncing twig; then he brought us up sharply, and we glided smoothly into a calm no longer than the canoe itself.

"Sam! Oh, Sam!" I sobbed. "Where are they?"

But he was watching every inch of water rushing past the entrance of our tiny haven. And then, as if by some miracle, Sam must have seen something. I was caught unawares when he shot the canoe into motion again. We leaped into the boiling water, and I felt him twist the canoe expertly.

"Left!" he shouted. I felt the muscles stand out on my back. Stretching my neck, I searched, hunting for a sign of dark head or bandit face.

"Right!" Sam shouted. "Now straightaway!" I heard his sharp gasp for breath. "There! George!"

I didn't see him till we were alongside. I ripped off my gloves and scooped Jacques out of the water. He was limp. His wet body was so tiny without the fluffiness of dry fur that he hardly looked like the same animal. I turned to Sam, but his teeth were set, his lips drawn back in a grimace of strain and fatigue. I looked up and saw the side of the cliff directly in front of my face. Sure that we would smash into it, I snatched up the paddle and pushed at the slimy rock, nearly losing the paddle. Sam shouted at me furiously, and we were off again.

"Sam, he's dead," I gasped.

"Get his head down. Squeeze his chest."

I tried to do as he said. I was trembling, and my hands were numb with cold.

"Roll him over," he shouted.

I did. I squeezed and relaxed, squeezed and relaxed. I guess maybe he did get up some water. Covering him, I tried to keep him warm. The rabbitskin robe was trailing alongside, and Sam flipped it in with the end of the paddle.

"He's dead!" I choked. "Oh, Sam. He's dead."

"Don't stop," he said fiercely. "Keep squeezing him. Blast! Blast!" And Sam went back to keeping us upright in the water.

So I had to give Jacques back his life. And I did, finally, after what seemed to be hours, though they really must have been only minutes. I felt the little ratlike body shudder, and although I couldn't feel his breathing I felt a change in him. In a moment he opened his eyes, and I felt one of the greatest reliefs of my life. I know I was half-blinded by tears when he tried to get to his feet, and I hugged him warmly against my chest.

And then the gorge, by some fluky upheaval of mother earth, widened for a few hundred yards. A tiny meadow that was the termination of a valley shot up in front of us. Sam got the canoe through a field of outcropping rocks and into a lee. For a moment we sat there in the shallows, still and grounded. I could hear him gasping to catch his breath, taking great lungfuls of air.

"Is—is he all right?" he asked, breathing hard.

"Yes. He's shivering, but he's all right. What of Ami?"

He shook his head. I could see the beads of perspiration standing out on his forehead. Already they were turning to ice as they froze. Then he motioned me ashore.

"But we can't leave Ami," I gasped.

Sam shook his head.

"Sam!" I breathed. "We might find him!"

He shook his head again. I could tell by his eyes the hurt went deep as his heart.

"Sam!"

"We can't, George. We've come far as we can go. The falls are a quarter mile below us."

My eyes widened in horror. "Oh, no," I whispered.

"Get out. We have to set up camp. Leave Jacques in the canoe till we have a fire."

I cooked the meal that night. As I sat by the little stove, smelling the stew, I wiped little bits of meat broth on Jacques' lips. He was terribly weak and couldn't seem to see properly. Sam told me he was lucky. Had we been a few seconds longer Jacques would not have survived.

Although we had stopped just after noon, it was dark a few hours later. The snow fell heavily and steadily, blotting out all that was left of the light. When Sam had seen me settled and the fire going, he had left. I didn't ask his chances of finding Ami. I know they would be small, and I didn't want to add to his anxiety.

After a few hours passed and he didn't return, I began to get fretful. The night was very cold; the wind had picked up and the moan of the tall trees was eerie. Finally in desperation I began the meal. Sam had told me not to attempt keeping a fire going outside, so I hadn't been out at all. Once, hours ago, I had opened the tent flap, but the scene outside scared me to death. I had barely been able to see the canoe tied to a tree.

"I knew this vacation was going to be awful," I said to Jacques between my chattering teeth. "And now we've lost Ami. If I ever, ever, get to Uncle Henry's, how in the blurry blue blazes will I get out of this country before the winter has me snowed in?" I shook my head hopelessly. This afternoon I had suddenly realized that we were fighting for our lives. The struggle wasn't fun; it was horrible, ugly, and I was dreadfully frightened.

And then the hair on my neck stood out. I stopped rubbing the blisters on my hands and wiped my tongue over my lips. There had come the very slightest of sounds, ones that weren't of the wind or snow. A step, a pad of feet, or was it only a rotten branch overheavy with snow that fell just outside. I cocked my head to one side and listened. Was that a crack of ice on the river? "Sam?" I whispered, gulping back my terror.

I opened the tent flap, pushing it back, and looked out on a most depressing sight—snow, darkness, and bitter cold. Light from the lantern cut only a piece out of the night. There wasn't anything at all, certainly not Ami or Sam. But somehow there was an alarming sensation of something being there. I did up the tent again. My hands were shaking when I went back to stirring the stew. I sat listening, calling up bits of unpleasant thoughts. Could it be wolves? I hated myself for being so frightened.

Hours later, when I had given up all hope of ever seeing Sam again, I heard him. I didn't wait for a call, but undid the tent and flung it wide. Looking like a white giant, he loomed up in front of me. He flopped his hands on his chest, legs, and arms, clearing the snow from himself as best he could. Then he stepped inside and took off his parka.

I couldn't speak. Obviously Sam hadn't found Ami. He must have been nearly frozen, and I had a cup of hot stew waiting for him.

The steam from the cup thawed the ice on his brows, and the water dripped down his nose. After a quick gulp, and then another, he looked up. "How's Jacques?"

I nodded, and Sam put his big hand on the sleeping raccoon.

"Ami?"

He shook his head. "He may have got ashore. I searched as far down as I could."

"Do you think he's all right?"

He shrugged. "If he got ashore before the falls."

"He did," I said absolutely. "He did!"

Sam slipped off his boots, and I handed him his mooseskin moccasins. Then he stretched out on the rabbitskin robe. Suddenly the tent became cozy and safe again. What was it— with his presence—that made all those little terrifying noises fade into nothing?

We spent a fitful night. Once I heard Sam get up and throw back the tent flap. I heard the click of the gun as he picked it up and knew he was looking out into the darkness. Pretending to be asleep, I lay straight as a stick, until at last the faint oily smell of metal came to me as Sam placed the gun between us and went back to bed. So my suspicions had been right—the sounds I heard had been wolves.

The snow was still falling the next morning and had drifted high against the canoe. Sam stood for a long time staring at the miserable scene around us. Then, as if he hadn't any choice, he told me to start breaking camp. But this time we didn't put all the gear in the canoe. We got into our backpacks. I objected that I could carry a heavier load, but Sam insisted that I take a light weight. The rest we stowed in the canoe.

I helped rig a line attached to the bow. Next we fashioned a rough sort of harness. One of us would pull the canoe over the snow like a cart horse. The other was to follow behind and lend a hand for a push if the going got rough. By the grim way Sam was working at the chore, I suspected it would get rough.

When it was light enough to see, we doused the lantern, put it with the other gear, and tucked the tarp around it all. Sam put on the harness.

"I hope you can find your way," I said nervously.

"Little worry about that," he said, looping the line over his shoulders. "We can only go one way—up."

"Up!" I said skeptically. "But don't we go down, around the falls?"

"No. First we have to cross the razorback. That's a fifteen-hundred-foot climb. And I might say, not the slightest bit gradual."

I peered at the heavy trees ahead. The dark bulk of mountain was not clearly visible, but it was there. I felt it.

"All set," he said, swinging the rifle over his shoulder. "Now George, don't hang back."

I went to my place at the stern. He put his back into getting the canoe in motion, and I shoved to help out. Nothing happened, and my heart sank like a stone. The canoe was so unbearably heavy it couldn't be budged. We would never get it over the mountain.

"Rock it back and forth," said Sam. "It's frozen in."

I pushed heavily, but my feet only skidded on the packed snow, and I slipped to my knees. I tried again, pushing and pulling, throwing my weight against the thing. Then Sam came to help. He put his shoulder against the bow and heaved. I heard the sharp crack of ice breaking, and the canoe moved ahead.

"Beef," he said to me. "You need more beef."

Irked, I went back to my position and shoved. The canoe moved like silk. We were going to get over the mountain after all.

We hadn't been under way very long when the appalling roar of the river shut off as if with a click of a switch. We were in dense forest, climbing steadily, and we couldn't see more than a few hundred feet ahead. The trees and brush were thick with snow, and in places the outcroppings of rocks were heavily drifted. In a matter of minutes our tracks disappeared from sight.

I spent most of my time flinching about to watch behind. Whether I expected to be attacked from the rear or whether I was looking for a sight of Ami's familiar dark shape, I wasn't sure.

We began to rise steeply and, from necessity, were going slowly. The footing was miserable. The trees thinned, and the rocks were becoming ledges and cliffs; I suspected we were above timberline. We were following a rift in the canyon, and probably, had it been summer, it would have been a gurgling little creek. Suddenly Sam slipped and toppled over like a felled tree. With the sudden slackening on the line the canoe stopped, then began to slip backward. I jammed my shoulder against it. But inch by inch, I began losing out. I dropped to my knees, dug in my toes, closed my eyes, and grimaced. Every ounce of my strength went into holding the canoe from sliding back down the mountain. I tried to call out, but couldn't summon a voice. When I was nearly ready to be run over by the canoe, Sam rushed up. He slipped a rock under the skeg holding it solidly. I sank stomach down in the snow gasping for breath.

"Kid," he chuckled. "You're red in the face."

I'd lost a moccasin in the deep snow, and by the time we found it my feet were so cold I had to wrap them in the rabbitskin to warm up. Sam was afraid that my toes might get frost-bitten.

"Are we near the top yet?" I asked, when we finally got under way again.

"We haven't even begun," he said, and succeeded in depressing me more than ever.

This part of the trip was an exhausting and difficult struggle. The cold tore into my lungs, and I was forever winded. Once when I had to stop for breath, Sam told me that we were nearly eleven thousand feet in elevation and bound to be breathless. The footing was so awful that one of us was forever picking himself out of the snow and stumbling back into place while the other held the canoe from zipping downhill like a rocket. My pack, which had seemed so foolishly light that morning, felt like lead. There were times I got so tired I simply slipped down on my knees and knelt gasping for breath, only to stagger on in a moment trying to help as much as I could. Sam was doing nearly all the work. He never seemed to get tired or falter. He would slip and slide, but never stopped to rest like myself. Seldom did he offer advice, except to cover my face or rub my nose and ears to be sure the circulation was there. We stopped often because of my feet, until finally he tore part of the rabbitskin into strips and wrapped them around my feet and legs.

Higher and higher we went. The snow got deeper, but, thankfully, the canoe glided smoothly over it. At last Sam stopped. He straightened his back, and keeping a strain on the line he pushed the canoe at right angles to the mountain. We relaxed, and I fell in the snow to get my breath.

"The top," he said.

I brushed the snow from my parka and looked out at the world. Long before I'd sucked myself into a shell like my turtle. I could see now it had stopped snowing. We certainly were at the summit, for we were perched on a narrow precipitous ridge. The sight was breathtaking. There below us were snow, trees, and the raging Long Arm. The river wound jerkily in and out of the gorge until it fell away, reappearing in the far distance.

"The Matasi," said Sam.

I had never been as close to a waterfall

before. It looked awfully big, and spray and mists rose up in a ghostly way through the trees around it. The way Sam looked at it bleakly, I suspected it was a wicked, killing place.

We set up a half-shelter with the tarp. Sam started the primus stove, and we made tea and hot soup. I think he would rather not have stopped, but I was nearly done in. Having something hot inside was the greatest difference ever.

When we started again down the opposite side of the ridge, we no longer had to pull the canoe. Instead we had the difficult job of holding the canoe back. Like some wild thing, the canoe seemed intent on skating down the rocky slope ahead of us. Sam shortened his harness lead and held to the gunwale. I helped by holding back at the hook of the stern. We kept skidding and slipping on our heels. Half the time we seemed to slide along on the seat of our pants. We were covering the distance twice as fast as we had in the morning.

"S—Sam." I was hugging the stern with my arms as if it might kick me off. He brought everything to a halt, throwing me slightly off balance, and I sat down heavily.

"S—Sam, I—I —" I was nervously looking over my shoulder "—Sam, I thought I saw something!" I crept to my knees and looked up the mountainside. The snow had begun to fall again, very slightly, and with the approaching twilight everything looked depressing and unfriendly. I shivered. Sam squinted and stared into the trees.

"I—I—for just a second—" I was shaking badly. "I saw something."

But Sam didn't move. He stood there staring, rooted like one of the big pines, until I wanted to scream. "No matter." He heaved me upright. "Have another couple miles to go. It will be dark before then if we don't get moving."

I pulled up the corner of the robe and peeped inside the canoe. Jacques was curled in a fluffy ball sleeping like a baby. My turtle was in the cooking pot, also sleeping. I lurched into motion as the canoe jerked me forward, and I started holding back with my shoulders, my hands on the rail. The way ahead descended even more steeply; we were following a sort of trail that was narrow and precipitous. Even Sam was beginning to gasp at the strain.

"How—how do you manage the portage alone?" I breathed at him.

"I carry the canoe on my back," he said shortly. I didn't see how, but by now I knew better than to tell him so.

Then Sam disappeared. The path we had been following had grown steadily narrower. The outside edge, where Sam was walking, fell away to a rocky bank and a treacherous drop. The canoe, on the inside, was nearly scraping the rocky face of the cliff. And just as it reached the narrowest part, Sam dropped out of sight. I let out a horrified sort of squeak. The canoe started to slide away from me. Somehow I managed to give the bow a yank and send it crashing into the cliff, where it stopped. Now I was afraid to move. The momentum of the stern had carried me to the edge, and I was perched precariously over a twenty-foot drop falling into a bed of sharp, daggerlike rocks. Even as I looked down, bits of snow caved off under my feet and smashed on them below.

"Don't move," Sam said quietly. He had caught himself from falling into that pit and clawed his way back up to the path. "Now give me your hand," he said, stretching out his arm. "Slowly."

I reached out to him. More snow fell from under my feet, and I stopped.

"Slowly," he said again calmly.

I could feel the perspiration pop out on my forehead. My heart was pounding, and my knees felt weak. When my hand finally touched his I felt a helpless relief, and as he grabbed my wrist I heaved a sigh. He gave one tremendous yank. I knew Sam was strong, but I hadn't realized he was capable of lifting me clear of the snow to fly through the air like a bird. I landed safely back on the trail where I got a stranglehold on a rock.

We retreated back from the treacherous section the way we had come, and when we could finally stop, we looked at the bow of the canoe. There was a nasty, ragged hole torn in the aluminum hull. "I'm sorry," I said. Such useless words struck me bitterly.

But Sam only clapped me on the shoulder. "Kid, if you hadn't pushed the canoe into the cliff, I'd not like to think what would have happened."

I puffed up slightly at his words and was just about ready to say something smart when I let out a little gasp and backed against the canoe, staring wide-eyed into the trees. My skin crawled. There were four of them, and even as I watched two more came up. Big, gray animals, twice the size of dogs, and I knew in an instant they were wolves. I felt Sam reach over the canoe and slip his rifle out from under the lashings.

"Chances are they won't come closer," he said, not at all ruffled.

There was one that looked as if he must be the leader. He was larger, meaner, more alert, and stood ahead of the others. I wished it wasn't snowing. I wished it wasn't nearly dusk. The shadows from the trees were long, the way ahead hazy and vague in the half-light.

"Probably game about," Sam said, not that the comment reassured me at all. "Take my place, George. I'll follow."

"How soon—where will we stop for the night?" I asked, getting into his harness.

He shook his head, then knelt to look again at the nasty hole in the canoe. "The river's not far, probably two miles. We can camp there."

"Two miles!"

Sam looked at me. "And if we don't get under way, we won't make it before full dark."

"What about them!"

He glanced back at the wolves. I was queasy just looking at them. Three were sitting down, but that big, ugly-looking leader had come closer. "It's their country," Sam said resignedly.

I really put my back into moving the canoe this time. We had to bypass that ugly mountainous stretch, and when we finally came to the easy slope leading to the river I nearly ran. I didn't want to watch behind us and yet was afraid not to do so. The wolves didn't go away; they just followed. They kept far enough back to be no great danger to us, but always close enough to be in sight. Each moment the darkness came nearer, and so did the wolves. Every now and then Sam stopped to gather wood and toss it into the canoe. Whenever any was within my reach I picked it up. We would need a big fire during the night, one that had to be fed from what was at hand. Sam wouldn't be able to leave me to gather anything—not with the wolves so near.

"Look!" I gasped.

Sam straightened up, looking at the tracks I pointed to in the snow.

"There's more of them in front of us!" I said frantically.

"These could be their tracks from earlier," he said.

I looked back at the wolves. "Sam, can't you shoot? You might hit one. Maybe the sound would frighten them away," I said fiercely.

He looked at me patiently, then sighed. "It won't do the least bit of good."

"Well, it might," I said nervously. I knew I was frightened and must be showing my fear.

I don't suppose the wolves were more than a hundred feet away and scattered through the low brush. That big one was standing beside an old broken pine. As Sam levered a shell into the chamber, I jumped, startled at the sound in the stillness. Then, as he raised the gun to sight, those wolves vanished like phantoms. There wasn't a one left, not a sign they had

been there. They might have been swallowed by the world.

"Oh," I said, my eyes big as saucers. "Oh!" So that was why he hadn't wanted to shoot. Now they were gone from sight. I swallowed and looked about the timber. Where, I wondered, would they be now? Sam eased the hammer forward and put on the safety. He looked at me, and he certainly didn't have to say a word "Oh fuss," I said bluntly. "Why didn't you tell me they would do that?"

He chuckled. "Well, next time you'll know."

We got the canoe in motion again, but I couldn't help checking behind us. "Are they still there?"

"Yes. You may see them if you look carefully, but they'll be wary now."

"I was almost beginning to like this country," I said. "I never will now."

"Well, don't blame it on the poor wolves. They're just doing what comes naturally. Did you know the Indians say timber wolves are the spirits of bad people who have come back to earth after they have died?"

"Oh, fine," I said. "I surely hope these aren't the worst of the crop." I bit my lip. "Will they attack?" I asked, hating myself for having to know.

Sam tucked the rifle under his arm and walked alongside me as I pulled the canoe. "I'll give you one worthy bit of advice. Never, ever, run from a wolf. Chances are there isn't one living that would attack anything if it turned and bluffed him out. Be different, of course, if he were starving, but these aren't. Bear in mind that a wolf can down a full-grown moose or eat a single deer at a meal. Can even break a man's leg with one crunch of its jaws. But it's panic that's on their side."

And as if those beasts were listening, from out of the twilight came the most spine-chilling wail I had ever heard. The big leader was on the fringes of the timber, his gray coat tipped with snow. His nose was pointed toward the sky, and he howled dismally and rather sadly. But before Sam could raise the rifle he was gone, out of sight and sound.

We camped below the falls. Although we couldn't see them, Sam said they were close enough. The trees were like magical figures, hung with icicles. The bushes were solid ice, and when I kicked them they tinkled and broke apart. The mists drifting down on us were already freezing.

The river was no longer a mad rushing thing, but glided past so slowly it hardly seemed the same Long Arm. It was wide and still, and Sam said it was very shallow in places. In the summer the trout fishing in the still pools was the very best in Canada, or so he thought. We built up two huge fires. Sam felled a rotten tree beside the tent, and we used it for more firewood. After we settled camp and got things in order, I started our meal. Sam lighted the lantern, examined the hole in the canoe, and started to work. But even beside the

big fire he had a difficult time. He was forever
having to stop and push his bare hands under
his armpits to warm them up. Finally, in desperation, he ran the bow of the canoe into the
tent, covered the remaining opening with our
heavy clothes, and worked inside.

Having the canoe in for a visit was very cozy.
Jacques felt so much better he had taken a short
stroll outside by the fire, though I wouldn't let
him go far. Now he was content to sit on the
point of the stem and watch Sam work under
his nose. Occasionally he reached down one
dark paw and patted him on the cheek.

There was a ragged tear in the aluminum
bottom about the size of a softball. I sat outside
the canoe and held a large round stone over the
hole while Sam tapped on the jagged edges
inside with the back of the ax. But even when
the hole was smooth, it was still big enough to
founder us in about a minute.

We had so few tools, certainly no nails or
screws, that I did not see how we could ever

make the canoe floatable again. But, as usual, I forgot about Sam's ability to cope with such problems.

He gave me one of his knives that had a screwdriver blade and put me to work again. The canoe had a thin wooden gunwale, on the inside of the hull, fastened with little aluminum bolts with screw heads. We had to take enough bolts off the gunwale to use to hold a patch on the hull. My job was awful. The bolts were pitted and impossible to free. My screwdriver was rickety and kept collapsing. On the inside the nuts were countersunk into the wood, and the pliers wouldn't fit into the holes. So before we could do any more Sam painstakingly carved enough wood away from each nut so the pliers would fit around it. Then while I unscrewed the bolt he kept it from turning. The chore was long and tedious.

When we finally got one out, we skipped along the gunwale, so as not to weaken it in one spot, and took out another. Finally we had ten bolts laid out like little jewels, and I waited for Sam to go on to the next step.

But the meal had cooked, so we stopped for it. I was able to make bannock fairly decently now, and my fish stew was even better than Sam's, which wasn't saying much. When we finished I put a tin of snow on to melt for tea, and we went back to the canoe.

Sam had a piece of leather left over from my moccasins. Measuring it over the hole, he cut from it a circle a good three inches larger than the opening. Next he sorted through a collection of thick, rough-looking wood slabs he had cut with the ax when he had chopped firewood. At last he found one that seemed to suit his specifications. He adjusted it on the inside of the canoe, this way and that, and when he got it just so, he began whittling it to fit the curve of the hull.

"I don't like to ask this," I said, "but how are you going to make holes in it for the bolts? You haven't a drill."

117

"The awl."

I raised my eyebrows, but knew better than to say his plan wasn't possible—for it was. After the wood was shaped, he put the sharp-pointed awl on the stove to heat. The first time he jabbed four times with the tip of the hot awl before a neat smooth hole appeared in the wood. Afterward, keeping the awl red-hot, he needed only three thrusts of the point. The holes were cleaner and neater than if he had done them with a drill, and he finished them nearly as quickly.

"Now you'll have to help again," he said, when the last hole was done. "Go outside and fetch a heavy piece of wood." I was back with a log before he had everything adjusted. "Now hold the butt of it over the hole on the outside. I'm going to punch through the holes and through the aluminum." He gave a whack with the ax. I felt the awl come through into the log. "Don't move it," he said, moving on to another hole. Whack! The next one went through.

Jacques jumped to my shoulder and stood with his hands on my head. Whack went the third, until all ten were finished.

"All right, so far," said Sam. "Hand me the lard."

"Lard?"

He spread the greasy stuff on both sides of the leather, then slapped it in place on the inside of the canoe. He aligned it on the bolt holes, and I held it. Next he greased the inside of the wood, got it in position on top of the leather patch, and shoved a bolt home. Everything fit like a charm.

"The lard will keep it waterproofed," he explained, setting all the bolts and nuts up tightly. The lard squeezed out the edges, and I could feel the canoe take on strength. The patch was so neat it was appalling.

"You are the handiest person to have about," I said, admiring the workmanship.

Sam smiled at me, his teeth shining white against his tanned face. Then he mussed my hair. "Could have done it yourself, if you had to, you know." I thought about that, wondering where I'd earned Sam's regard.

"All we need," I said wistfully, "is Ami. Do you think he might be alive?"

I'd surely put a damper on things with that remark. Sam shrugged and opened the tent. It was so snug and cozy I rather hated to have him shove the canoe back outside. The campfire was burning low, the embers glowing. A little spiral of smoke weaved overhead.

"Oh, look!" I gasped.

The stars had come out. The clouds were gone. Somewhere to the east the moon was rising, and the world was a glistening mackerel silver.

"The stars are like diamonds," I said.

"These blessed candles of the night," said Sam, tossing a few shreds of leftover leather into the fire. Sparks shot up with a crackle, and the clean piney smell of woodsmoke came to me. I turned to look at him—a long, thoughtful look.

"That's from *The Merchant of Venice*," he said dryly. "Act Five."

So we sat there in the ice and snow and watched the stars, until finally I caught Jacques up around his middle and went back to my cup of tea. No need explaining to Sam how much I had come to like the high country. I suspected he already knew.

CHAPTER FOUR
End of the Trail

The next morning dawned clear as a bell and, unfortunately, cold as the polar ice cap. In fact, the river had frozen over. I had walked down to scoop up a tin of water and stood there gaping at it like a fool until Sam appeared. He said a few unprintable words, then jammed the butt of the gun on the ice. He succeeded in cracking it just enough for me to pry out the pieces and get to the water.

So we couldn't paddle after all. Instead, we walked along the edge of the bank on the river ice, towing the canoe. Jacques was feeling better and sat like a figurehead in his special perching place. Occasionally I plucked a few tender shoots punching above the ice for my turtle. Though he seemed content to stay in the bottom of the canoe, it was cold, so I'd taken to letting him ride in the cooking pot. Sam kept saying that we might have turtle soup by accident some night, but I knew he was joking.

We made good time. After all, we were traveling on flat ground. Toward noontime the sun actually got so warm I unbuttoned my jacket. Sam had his fur parka thrown back. Then in a few hours we stopped. "Ice is getting weak," said Sam shortly. "We'll have to go more slowly and stay close to the bank. And get that fool raccoon away from that patch!"

I took Jacques by the scruff of the neck and scolded him. He was licking and chewing at the raw edge of the leather. The lard Sam had put on it must have tasted delicious.

But we couldn't stay as close to the bank as we wished. The country had changed drastically. Instead of being enclosed by the slippery cliffs of the gorge above the falls, the river was now the center of a wide thickly wooded valley. Edging the river were huge oaks and ashes, willows and aspen. Bamboo and bullrushes kept us from telling exactly where the bank began. Sam said this part of the country was a big swampland in the summer, and the beavers had built so many dams in the area that it was nearly a lake. Surrounding us were always the great mountains. They gave me the feeling that we were trapped in the bottom of a cup. There seemed to be no way out.

Suddenly the quiet of the afternoon was shattered by a sharp, riflelike explosion, and I stopped in my tracks. The canoe skated to a halt, and I looked up to Sam. He had been walking ahead testing the ice and was now standing very still, carved awkwardly into place like a silly child playing the game of freeze. A great rift in the ice had opened, and black, sucking water was almost directly beneath his feet.

"Sam!" I whispered. He was going to go in! Quickly I took off my harness and untied the

bitter end from the canoe. "I've my line free," I said. "Shall I toss it to you?"

"Yes. But don't come much closer, and don't move quickly."

I slipped off my pack and moved toward him. He wasn't, I suspected, more than twenty yards away, and I had crossed about half that when another sharp crack stopped me. I gasped. Sam tried to move backwards, but as he did the ice began to break up.

Sam was in a very deadly spot. I noticed for the first time how the river had begun to narrow as we approached a sharp bend. I could imagine the current just beneath his feet and how easily it could pull him under. Cautiously I moved forward, until I felt the rubbery, unpleasant sway of the thinning ice. I swallowed. "I—I think the line will reach."

"I can't move, George," he said calmly, as if he was in this situation every day of his life. "If I do, I'm apt to go down."

I coiled the line in my hand, trying to remember the proper way to toss it. It fell short the first time, knotted in a wad of kinks. I could feel the sweat standing out on my forehead. I tried again, and it fell directly on his arm. He crooked his elbow, and the end slipped into his hand.

"Now take it over and tie it."

There was a broken tree jutting out just above the ice and snow on what looked like a substantial bank. I looped the line over a branch and made it fast.

Sam slowly took up the strain. Then, with a sudden jerking motion, twisted himself about and ran. Without the line to help him he would never have been able to reach the bank. The ice where he had been standing shattered in a hundred pieces. At each of his steps it groaned and crackled, and as soon as he picked up a foot it broke. Sam's dash was a mad sort of game—playing tag with disaster. I held my breath as I waited to see if he could gather in the slack line and give himself the momentum he needed before the ice completely sucked him under. Then he leaped ashore, past the bullrushes and willows, and stood in the snow beside me. He grinned.

"T-that was mighty neat footwork," I said shakily.

"Track team, you know," he said lightly, then put his hand on my shoulder. "Thanks for your help, friend."

I grinned. "Sure, any time," I said smartly.

"Well." He waved his hand at the river. "No more of that. I rather think the ice has broken up around the bend. Let's get going and find out."

Sam was right. The change was startling, like turning a page of a book. Not only did the ice on the river disappear abruptly, the snow cover on the ground dwindled into patches and finally gave way to the bright green of grass and scattered trees. The meadow in the distance looked warm and delightful.

We had a nervous moment when we

launched the canoe for the first time, and the patch sank beneath the water. I glued my eyes to it, looking for leaks, but Sam only chuckled. "Dry as a bone," he said. "But will you *please* —" he picked up Jacques and shoved him in my arms "—keep him from eating it up."

We loaded the canoe, and Sam took his usual place at the stern paddle. I hesitated by the bank.

"What's the matter?" he asked.

"If only Ami would suddenly burst out of those woods and come back."

I could see the pain flash in his eyes for an instant. "No hope, I'm afraid."

"But to leave him. . . ."

"If Ami is alive, he can manage alone. We've made this trip down to your uncle's a few times; he might even head for there."

"I feel like a murderer," I said.

"Survival is a part of the high country," he said, as I stepped into the canoe. "You come to accept it after a while."

I only shook my head.

"And—" he looked at Jacques on the tip of the bow—"that brings me to the unpleasant chore of tossing him out to cope."

Every nerve in my body tensed. "Oh, Sam," I begged. "No!"

"No, I can't abandon him any more than you. Why do I always get myself mixed up in things like this?" He sighed and got us started down the stream.

Only a few hours later the shocking brutality of the high country came to us again. We happened to see a trampled path through the swamp grass and the great dark bulky thing lying on the stones of the riverbank. Sam came closer to look, and I wished he hadn't. A dead moose, mauled and half-eaten, was lying there.

"Wolves," Sam said unpleasantly. "We must have frightened them off. There! By the trees."

That big gray leader and his pack had returned. I looked at the bloody mangled mess on the beach and was glad we were in the canoe. "Please," I said, "do we have to look at it?"

Sam back paddled and got us out into the main current. In a few minutes we turned a crook in the river, and the scene was behind us. The mountains, the trees, the loveliness of the river, and the canoe swallowed up the ugliness.

We camped early. Now that the snow was gone Sam wanted to hunt for some sort of small game for a meal before dark. He built up a big fire, and I helped gather firewood. Next I was lectured. At sight of wolves I was to get into the canoe and paddle into the mainstream. A wolf, he told me, wouldn't be caught wet unless absolutely necessary. Besides, with an empty canoe, I could easily outdistance any animal swimming.

So with that happy farewell Sam tramped off into the trees and left me fidgeting at the fireside. The cold was not as intense as it had been the past few days, and since it was still light I didn't want to go in the tent. Sam explained that we had been losing altitude steadily, and with each foot the weather ought to improve. However, he hastened to add that winter was coming. Although the weather was decent enough today, it could worsen any minute.

After about an hour I thought I saw a movement out of the corner of my eye. I looked around nervously, but there wasn't a thing in sight. However, I had certainly succeeded in making myself jittery. I kept looking about for that pack of timber wolves. Surely they wouldn't have come this far downriver when we had seen them at the carcass of the moose. No need wishing so, I knew well enough they could travel a hundred miles in a day if they wanted.

Then I saw it again—the flicker of movement that had caught my eye. It was a rustle in the grass beneath an ancient tree. I heaved a sigh of relief. Under no circumstances could a wolf fit in that cropped bit of green. And then I saw it clearly—a flutter of wings.

"Oh," I said irritably, "it's only a bird." It acted as though it was caught or perhaps sick. I stalked over to the patch of grass big as life, but I kept my eye on the canoe, too, judging how far I would have to run if I saw danger coming over the ridge.

The motion certainly was a bird, and there wasn't anything wrong with it at all. Its only problem was that it hadn't grown large enough to leave its nest. It was just a baby, and an owl at that. I caught it up in my hand, then let out a howl as it bit my thumb. I dropped it again. For a minute I was more concerned about my finger, which felt as if it had been bitten clean off, than the fool bird. But finally after making some cooing sounds I picked it up, and it seemed to take to me right off.

"Hey, you're cute," I said, and looked at the top of the old, weathered tree. "I suspect you came from that hole up there."

I nursed my finger and tried to figure out a way to get that baby owl back up there short of my taking him. The hole was about twenty-five feet up, and there were no low branches. I didn't like the way they were spaced below the entrance either; I might well meet an indignant mother owl when I was busy with handholds.

I considered leaving him alone. But he was awfully small and helpless despite that knife-like beak. I cooed some more. "Poor little guy."

I knew I was licked. First I took off my jacket and hood, and tucked my gloves in my pocket. Then I shinnied up a ways; it wasn't the least bit easy, and I could have used a boost for a start.

The climb was slow and splintery. The sap oozing from the tree was like glue; I'd be sticking to everything for a month. I snaked a leg over the limb and readjusted the owl. If ever there's an awkward spot it's upside-down, swinging like an ape, trying to get a decent grip on a finger-eating owl. I guess I wasn't cooing enough, because the owl kept biting me. "Ow. Ow!" I stuck him roughly in my sweater pocket. But he bit through and nipped me on the stomach. "Yow!"

I was going to wring his neck in a minute. However, I managed to get my muffler over his beak. Although he might well be suffocated by the time I got to the top, at least I wouldn't be a bloody shred. I carefully tested my weight on the branches and made my way up. Not being especially keen on heights, I imagined the ground below was twenty times farther away than it really was. Once I put my foot on a bleached limb, and it cracked off directly under me. If I hadn't had my other hand free, I'd have fallen. I managed the last few feet, and, taking hold of the nearest branch with one hand, I jammed the owl with the other—none too gently—into the nest.

I came down slower than I had come up, and more than once rotten branches broke under me. At last I jumped the remaining few feet and landed safely on the ground. I brushed at the dirt and pine needles on my sweater. Then I stood there gawking suspiciously at another little gray owl like the one I'd just put in the nest. It came staggering out of a hole in the base of the old tree.

"Oh, great." I bent over and looked inside the tree. The owl was the same one all right. The tree was hollow. He had simply come flopping back down the inside when I'd stuffed him in at the top. "Well, the next time you can take the elevator," I said shortly. I had to laugh; he surely was a funny one. His quick trip down the inside of the tree had left him dusky and smudged, and his feathers were ruffled. He looked so ridiculous I couldn't help but smile at him. Even his two little feather horns were out of place, and he had the appearance of an upset devil. I smoothed his feathers, and he promptly turned to me with his mouth open and screeched. The noise was awful—not bird-like or pretty at all.

"Glory!" I exclaimed, shocked. Then when I recovered from the blast, I said, "I'll bet you're just hungry." And he certainly was. He wasn't mean or vicious; he wanted something to eat.

I took him into the tent and got a piece of goose meat from the supplies. The first chunk I gave him was too big, and he didn't know what to make of it. Even when I shredded it and put it in front of him, he still wouldn't eat. But then I took it in my fingers and held it out, which made the difference. I was now apparently classed as his mother. He gobbled up the meat and began squeaking for more—not nearly so loudly this time, and more pleasant to the ear. Jacques came up to see what was going on and sat beside me. He yawned and looked at the little bird sleepily. Then he smelled the meat and begged for a bite, irritating the little owl. He must have been an only child. Huffing himself up to nearly twice his size, he arched his wings and let go with a loud *hoo-hoo!* He looked so fierce that I nearly died laughing.

"Oh, you silly baby," I choked.

Jacques didn't think he was a silly baby. He ran for my shoulder and hid behind my neck quivering.

Suddenly the tent flap flew back, and Sam shoved his head inside. He was frowning unpleasantly. "I thought you were going to stay by the canoe."

"Sam, look," I said. "He fell out of the tree."

Sam perked up slightly. "At least you did better than I did."

The owl was eating again. I carefully broke up the meat and handed it to him. His table manners were not very polite. He got the food in his mouth, gulped, blinked, and opened up for more. He seemed to be unfillable.

"Hey," said Sam. "That's not our goose meat!"

"Just a morsel." I stroked the owl's feathers.

"Well, let's not overdo fattening up the lamb." He took the rest away from me and re-wrapped it. "Were there any more?"

"No. Only him."

"Too bad. One won't be very much."

I looked up horrified, then clutched the bird to my heart. "Sam!"

He was taking off his jacket and stopped with it halfway over his head. "What's the matter?"

"You—oh, you wouldn't *eat* him."

"For pity's sake," he said irritably. "An owl is as good as a chicken. I'm tired of fish and dried goose meat."

"But—but he's just a baby!"

Sam looked at me thoughtfully. "What happened to you?"

"I fought with the tree."

"You look as if you lost," he said crossly. Then he glanced sourly at the owl. "Well, since we can't have you for soup, do you mind if I start up some goose stew before that's all gone?"

That night Sam told me about the sort of plane he would buy to replace the one we had lost. He wanted a sea plane this time, with pontoons for the lakes. He told me about the hunters who loved to go deep into the high country, and of the cabin he had built on the edge of an emerald lake. Someday he wanted to show it to me.

Sam also talked about Ami, of the time he had been a puppy nine years before. He sat by the stove stroking Jacques. I was brushing the feathers of Little Huff—a proper name I had given him, I thought. He was perched on the rifle stock and looked sleepy-eyed and content. Then Sam took out the maps, and we looked over our location.

"So close," I said excitedly. "We'll get there tomorrow, won't we?"

He yawned. "What a shock you'll give Henry. You look like a wild Indian."

I grinned. Sam couldn't have given me a nicer compliment.

After we went to bed, I lay thinking about seeing Uncle Henry and Aunt Min. I wondered if they would send me right off again, or if by some unlikely chance it would begin to snow. Wouldn't that be a piece of grand luck to be snowed in for the winter? Then I wouldn't have to say good-bye to Jacques or search up a home for Huff. I'd even be able to keep old turtle. Uncle Henry would be a stickler for school, but I could always use his books to study. I squirmed with pleasure. Then I caught myself; I remembered how much I had fought against coming to the high country, and I chuckled.

I heard the soft pad of Jacques' feet on the tent floor. He was restless, but finally settled himself, soft and warm, beside my hand. Then I heard a faint *hoo* from Little Huff, who was wide-awake, hopping around everywhere. The turtle was eating away on a bullrush and making moist, grinding noises. I would miss them all terribly if I had to go right back.

The next day the weather was sparkling bright, almost as warm and pleasant as summer. Standing by the fire, Sam looked up at the clouds forming over the peaks. He sucked in great lungfuls of air and said he was thankful we could make Uncle Henry's today. A roaring good snow was on its way.

Our valley was like a Christmas card—all snow and mountains and big green trees. I sipped my tea beside Sam and watched a big, eight-point buck and four does grazing within sight. Then I ambled down to the river to throw stones. I had Little Huff on my arm and could feel the sharpness of his talons as he gripped my jacket. When I got to the water I put him on a branch of a toppled pine and proceeded to search about for some skimming rocks.

Suddenly there was a horrible scream from Huff, and I jumped so awkwardly I nearly fell into the river. There was a mad thrash of wings directly in my face. The idiot was simply trying to fly to me, and once in the air didn't know where, or how, to land. Every time I made a motion to catch him he shrieked as if he'd been strangled. I could tell he was nearly at his wits'

end. He simply didn't know how to land on my outstretched arm.

"Oh, you dope," I said foolishly. "Just fold up." But there was no use talking to a frustrated owl. He hooed again, and then again, flapping higher in the air. I was running around beneath him as if I'd lost my senses, too.

"Not over the water, not over the water," I chanted. But no use. Little Huff was exhausted, and with a few last feeble attempts to fly he gave up completely. He went into a tailspin, disappearing into the river.

"Oh, no," I gasped. "Oh, no! Sam!" I screamed. "Sam! Help!"

In a moment Sam bolted out of the brush. He had the rifle in his hand and a grim, fierce look on his face. When he saw me, he stopped short and let out his breath with a puff. "What the devil were you bellowing about?"

I grabbed him by the jacket. "Over there," I sobbed. "It's Little Huff."

I could just make out the owl flopping half

in, half out of the water near the opposite side of the stream. He looked more in than out, though, and if we didn't hurry he would drown. "Sam, please help," I pleaded.

The canoe was heavy, but I don't remember our lifting it to the water. Sam jumped in so quickly he left me behind. He crossed to the opposite side in a second, reached into the river, and scooped up the owl. When he shouted back, I made out that Little Huff was all right. Sam was shaking his head and muttering.

Hastily I went back to camp. I was going to be in for a lecture, and I wasn't anxious to hear it. Besides, Sam was tired; he hadn't slept well last night. Huff had kept hopping and hooing about.

But when I got to camp I couldn't find Jacques, and the dreadful thought came to me that he might have wandered off and gone back to the land where he truly belonged. I started calling him, although I knew he wasn't likely to listen if he was out for a prowl. Then I took a piece of his favorite dried fish from the camp supplies, stuffed it in my pocket, and set out to look for him.

The logical place for him to be was by the water, but I'd just come from there and hadn't seen him. Besides, I wasn't anxious to meet Sam and Little Huff until they had settled down to be friends. Sometimes Jacques went into the trees and turned over old logs and leaf mold looking for worms. So, pretending I was a raccoon, I started for the choicest-looking grubbing spot.

Everything was lovely; the grass was warm, the smell of the trees and the snow breeze was sweet and clean. The tang of woodsmoke from our fire was nearly good enough to eat. I passed the spot where the deer had been grazing and stopped to examine a toadstool, or could it be a mushroom. Had it been knocked over by a hoof or a little paw? I bent to look, feeling like an old woodsman. Not a hoof. Jacques must have been tasting it. Yes, there were some long scratches on the dark earth. Next I found a rotten limb newly turned. I whistled softly. "Jacques?"

He had really dug up a hole there. And farther on, by the deeper trees, another limb was upended. Where was the little beast? He seldom strayed from camp since he had been nearly drowned in the river. I made a little click of annoyance with my tongue and walked on up to the edge of the forest. The limb that had been turned was larger than it had looked in the distance. I studied it thoughtfully. Ants were still creeping over it, and a little white, maggotlike worm was slithering into a pitted piece of bark. Surely this spot was freshly dug up. I tugged, using both hands and nearly all my weight before it rolled back in place with a clunk.

I finally realized that the track I'd been following hadn't been Jacques'. Slowly I turned around, wiping my tongue over my lips. Camp was a devilishly long way away, and as I watched I saw Sam just coming up the path from the river. He was carrying Little Huff and probably talking to him.

Then I heard a rattle of brush a few feet away. It was thick scrub, and as my eyes focused on it directly I saw it was heavy with berries. I couldn't move just then; I was paralyzed with fright. But I hadn't time anyway. There was a crash of branches; the bush parted and from behind it tumbled a brown bundle that rolled over like a rubber ball. Then another one flew out and rolled beside the first, and both ended up almost directly under my feet. When they stopped bouncing, I saw that they weren't little fur balls at all, but bear cubs.

If ever I was to have a failing of heart, I think that moment would have been it. I wasn't the least bit worried about these two, though they weren't rightly what I would call tiny bundles of fluffy joy. Both of them probably outweighed me. What terrified me and kept me rooted to the ground was their mother. I wasn't so foolish that I didn't know where my danger would come from.

The two cubs must have thought I was a tree. They didn't act as though they suspected I was about, and soon I knew why. A waft of icy wind coming from the highest mountains hit my face. They obviously didn't have my scent. I took a step back. If I could get away before the mother identified me, I might get to camp, or at least within sight of Sam. I took another step, and then another. One of the cubs looked up as my foot snapped a rotten twig. He stopped boxing his brother's face with some ugly-looking paws and looked me over. The way he waved his head about gave me the impression that his eyesight was a bit poor. Actually, he was trying to pick up my smell. Then he squatted far back on his haunches like a fat pig and watched me curiously over his stomach.

I started to sweat; I could feel beads of perspiration running down my armpits. My heart was pounding. The cub's attention went to his toenail, and he bit at it. I took another step backward. The other cub looked up, and I froze. I still couldn't see their mother, though now I heard a loud ripping noise, probably she was clawing up broken stumps. The cubs heard it too and began swatting each other again. I took two more steps back, and as I did both cubs caught my scent. They stopped playing instantly and let out a terrified roar. For one ghastly second I steeled myself not to run. I knew if I did, I'd probably never run again.

Then the mother bear erupted through the blackberries like a tank bursting out of the jungle. I gasped. She was as black as the inkiest night and gleamed like velvet. Her snout was huge and long. She took one look at me and let out a bellow that could have been heard a hundred miles away. My spirits sank to the lowest ebb ever.

There wasn't a tree in sight to climb, nor

anywhere to run. Camp was a million miles away, or so it seemed. Actually I didn't know what to do. Once the mother bear saw the two cubs, and they rolled into her safely, she stopped roaring and stood beside them protectively, glaring at me. She was so near that I could see the leaves from the bushes stuck to her forelegs. Perhaps if she realized that I was trying to retreat she might let me alone or, better yet, take her family and go.

I took another step backward. It was the wrong thing to do. Looking seven feet tall and apparently weighing a ton, she reared back on her hind legs. Her feet, with those long, deadly-looking curved claws, could probably cut me in pieces with one swipe.

The cubs crept under the bushes and disappeared, but she wasn't about to follow them. I was shaking so badly I could hardly breathe. Clasping my hands to my sides, I felt the little packet of fish I'd brought for Jacques. I took it out and tossed it to the ground.

But the mother bear wasn't hungry at all. She let out another roar, and at the same moment I heard the crack of a rifle. Sam must be coming. She dropped on all fours again and looked hesitantly after her cubs. I took another step backward. She reared again, this time her great jaws opened wide, and I could see the dirty yellowness of her teeth. She was enough to make one die of fright. I took another step back. She weaved forward. I didn't wait another second. I turned tail and ran like the wind.

I didn't get more than my own length anyway, when I stumbled over Jacques and went down in a heap. He must have been looking for me. One of us let out a squeal, and I rolled over as the bear came for me.

I saw a black blur, which I thought was one of her cubs. It flew at her haunches, jarring her out of stride. I scrambled to my feet and caught a glimpse of black again. This time it was at her other side. It was roaring and snarling almost as loudly as the mother bear.

153

Glory! It was Ami! Ami who was supposed to be drowned and lying dead along the riverbank. There was another shot, and I nearly leaped out of my skin. "No! No!" I screamed, as I ran across the meadow toward Sam. "It's Ami!"

But I was so breathless that he probably could not hear me. He had the rifle up and pressed to his shoulder. I ran like a deer and leaped at the gun barrel. As I shoved it to one side Sam lost his balance. Then, far away, I heard another shot.

"It's Ami!" I screamed at Sam again. "Don't shoot!"

There was a sudden squeal of a dog, and Sam's mouth dropped open. We both stared across the meadow. There was a man—no two, and one was firing into the air. Both the bear and the dog had stopped and were looking at them. The man fired again. This time dirt shot up under the bear's nose and flew in her eyes. Ami made a quick nip at her haunches. She swung at him, missing him by inches, but the dog was too fast for her. But now the mother bear was concerned only for her cubs. She gave one horrendous roar, ran into the thicket, and was gone.

Ami nearly turned a somersault in midair and came toward us like a black cyclone. He leaped directly into Sam's arms, and the two of them fell flat on the grass. The two people came jogging across the meadow to meet us.

"It's Uncle Henry!" I said stupidly. "Aunt Min!"

The reunion was lovely, everyone shaking hands and kissing everybody else. Little Huff bit Uncle Henry on the finger, and he started to shout. Then Jacques came up, trembling. But the lot of us were nearly loved alive by Ami. He looked big and fat and healthy. We were ever so glad to see him.

"Oh, Sam," I said. "I knew he would come back."

"Man, that dog's been the most unpleasant company," said Uncle Henry with a laugh. "He

came in three days ago and wouldn't let us be
till we came out after you."

Aunt Min scratched Jacques on the nose, and
he nearly purred in ecstasy. "We waited till
today and had to come. Henry figured something must have happened to the plane. Good-
ness, George, you and Sam are the nicest
persons we ever hoped to see."

Ami was whirling around like an idiot, and
Sam was nearly as happy as he was. Then he
sobered. "Say, you nearly scared me to death!"
he said to me.

I grinned and scooped up Jacques.

We broke camp and loaded the canoe. For
the final time, we folded the line tent and buried
our fire. Uncle Henry looked a little unsure
about the canoe holding all of us, but Sam
said so much had happened to us one more
sinking wouldn't matter. I took the bow paddle,
and Uncle Henry and Aunt Min faced each
other as if they were going to play pat-a-cake.
They were laughing so much they shook the

canoe. Sam took the stern paddle and with an effort got us pushed off from shore. We hadn't much freeboard, but still we floated. I had the owl on my shoulder, tied down with a leather shoelace on his ankle. Ami was curled just behind me, leaning against my back. And, as usual, our figurehead was Jacques. My turtle was up taking the time of day on the pile of packs.

Uncle Henry laughed. "I say, this looks like the Ark."

I took one last look across the meadow wondering if the mother bear had settled back to a more enjoyable humor. I felt a little pang of heartache as Sam brought us out to the mainstream of the Long Arm and the canoe picked up the speed of an arrow.

"Sam," I said, "remember a long time ago I told you I hated this place."

"Yes. It was only a week ago."

"You said someday I wouldn't hate it."

He chuckled.

"You were right—I don't hate it. I guess I love it as much as you do." I turned to smile at him, and then at Uncle Henry and Aunt Min.

"Oh, dear," said Aunt Min. "I almost hope you won't be able to get out before the snows come. They are so early this year. What fun we could all have."

I perked up.

"Never be able to make it out," said Uncle Henry, grinning. "Never make it. You'll just have to miss this semester of school, I'm afraid, George."

I turned off my brain and puffed up with happiness. And to add to everything it was starting to snow—big heavy flakes that would soon fill up the high country. I swiveled about to look at Sam, and he winked at me slyly. Not to be outdone, Little Huff bit me on my ear.

About the Author

Born in Nebraska and educated in California, Marian Rumsey is a travel enthusiast. Some years ago she and her husband and two children completed a cruise around the world, which included a year's stopover in the Hawaiian Islands. They live aboard a forty-foot sailboat, the *Black Dolphin,* and, since they travel continually, cannot call any one city or state their home. They next plan to go to the South Pacific and Australia. Mrs. Rumsey has written many articles about the family cruises and is well known in boating and yachting circles. She also writes general travel articles in addition to her children's books.